The Flight

Of The

Magician

A NOVEL BY

MARK SNOW

Dedicated to Mo, because she said so.

CHAPTER 1

My Sleep Disorder

Here's a childhood flashback – when I used to wake up scared, when there were unseen monsters under the bed or in the closet, I would perform a ritual that would clear my bedroom of any invisible bad spirits. I'd get out of bed and turn on the lights. Then, I'd spread my arms wide and sweep the room while the imaginary phantasms, devils, and monsters would scurry away or be pushed out the door. I would imagine myself being fearless and powerful, so those things wouldn't want to hassle with me or want to come back.

I was very thorough. I made sure I covered all the corners, spaces, and in-between areas in my room. The space between the bunk beds, under the bed, the closet, behind the door... everywhere. With a drowsy yet measured pace and outstretched arms, I would herd all those invisible baddies out of my room. Sometimes, I would even think a double sweep was necessary. It made me believe I was safe and in-charge so I'd forget about spirits or whatever was lurking or bothering me. I'm sure, at the time, the procedure was probably enough to tire me out and reassuring enough so I could fall asleep again. Then back into bed, I'd crawl. With covers up to my nose, I'd feel safe, in control, and go back to sleep. For my younger self, a kid, it worked every time.

But now, tonight, I've woken up, again. Dammit! I'm tired of being tired. And it's been happening far too often lately. Something woke me and although I need to sleep, I'm awake and my head is pounding. I can feel my sweaty veins popping up on the sides of my head with the regular surge every heartbeat. What the hell time is it anyway? "Hello Irma," I say out loud. (It's my "hands-free" clock.) "Good morning," it answered. "Irma, time?" I command. "It's 3:13 am" Crap... fricking great. Now I'll be exhausted tomorrow. And I'm still tired.

These covers, they're way too hot. Naked or clothed, in pajamas, or half-dressed. It doesn't seem to matter, I still wake up sweating. No wonder I drink myself into bed most nights. Not hardcore drunk but enough to buzz me into an alcohol assisted sleep. As I gather my senses I see around my bedroom that beer cans seem to be self-populating everywhere. And, they're occasionally overseen by a taller rum or vodka bottle on the dresser or nightstand. They stand in stark contrast to my otherwise spartan and well-ordered bedroom. Why do I let those things accumulate? And, what in the hell is that noise? What is it that woke me up this time? I lift my head off my pillow to get an idea of where it's coming from. I hear - Beeezz, beeez, click... click, click. "Aaaah shit," I say to myself. That's a way too familiar sound. It's coming from the kitchen. The damn ice maker has frozen solid in the freezer again. It's made itself into a frozen log jam of ice chunks. I thought for sure it was closed earlier.

My mind races back to me making a drink and pushing the freezer door closed just before going to bed. I know I closed it. However, it MUST have been left open. Did I leave it open? Dammit. And, how many times has this happened lately? Dozens I think? The actual count is probably much higher. That's very much not like me. I know I'm not one to leave things open. Closet doors, dresser drawers, fridge doors, caps on toothpaste, etc. I'm adamant about things like that. Things need to be put-right and returned to as they should be, corrected, fixed, in their rightful place, working properly, and looking tidy. And although it can be an obsession, I like things to be in order.

The desire to rectify things lends me to a compulsion to fix and repair. I love fixing stuff. Although, I sometimes think to my-self that - fixing things might be a minor curse in my life. I can fix anything. Well, nearly anything. I think it's because I love to know how things work. Why throw it away if you can fix it? And, if I see something that needs to be fixed, it's hard not to jump right in and do it. Because of my mad obsession to make it right, precious time is used, sometimes wasted, fixing. Even when it could be more cost-effective to replace or just toss it. It often wastes time, yet simultaneously, can be proudly satisfy-ing.

So here I lay in bed. Listening to that buzz, buzz, click, click. It's going to last forever until something is done about it. I defin-itely won't get back to sleep knowing that the ice maker is not right. You know, I've got to fix, so up I go into the kitchen and to the freezer to dump a frozen solid, half-full, ice-maker tray of ice and congealed cubes into the sink. Next, I pour hot water in the ice tray to melt away the little ice bits that are stuck there. When the freezer door is open it will slowly but eventu-ally close on its own. But then the maker will refreeze and cause a jam. Thus the confounded buzz/click that drives me crazy, and tonight wakes me up. As always, it's probably because the freezer door wasn't fully closed, oddly enough, again. Strange.

I clear out the ice maker and let the refrigerator go back to doing its thing. Ok, finally, that's done. Truth is, I'd rather be sleep-ing right now. Meanwhile, during all this, I realize my head still hurts. Since I'm up and in the kitchen, I tidy up the kitchen a bit, throw away a few empty beer cans only to find one that is full, warm, and open. Dammit! I do hate wasting anything. Being a single guy, coming from modest upbringings, anything wasted is money lost. And who likes wasting money? Wasting money, beer, anything, upsets me. And, a full warm beer seems to be a double pity. Oh well, nothing to be done about it now, down-the-sink-it-goes.

In preparation to get back to bed, I go to the fridge, open and down a fresh cold beer in its entirety. "There, that should work." I've come to depend on the depressive qualities of alcohol to work its magic. Now it's back to bed and hopefully, sleep. Sweet, sweet sleep.

I wake up again this night with a start. It feels like only minutes since I fell asleep. I'm feeling uneasy. It's as if someone or something is watching me. I lay still and listen. I don't hear anything. Did something move? Is it that damn ice maker again? Everything is quite. It's dead quiet. Maybe I was having a bad dream. I've always been somewhat plagued by them, beginning way back as a kid. I try to remember what I watched on TV last. Maybe thoughts of that woke me up, but I can't remember. I don't think that was it, however, something woke me up. If it was a nightmare, over the years I've learned how to deal with them.

My reaction has been, to believe in the power of positive thoughts. So much so that I'd try and redirect my dreams, even my nightmares, when I needed to. Especially the nightmares. I'll take the negative thinking and understand they are mine, my thoughts, that are causing anxiety. And since they are, after all, MY thoughts, then it's up to me to change them. I try to dispel or redirect the negative direction my mind is taking and steer towards positive thoughts and emotions.

Then, with mental conviction, I'll flood my head with enough good ideas that I will eventually allow myself to get back to sleep. I'll try, with positive thoughts, to think away my demons/spirits/bad thoughts... whatever is bothering me, whatever is interrupting my night. But now tonight, again, only minutes since the ice maker incident. I've had another unsettling, interrupted, middle-of-the-night awakening. However, this time something feels a little different.

Something had moved, I'm sure of it. Something soft, imperceptible, like the sound of a person hanging a coat jacket in a closet. A movement that was noiselessly quiet. I also feel hot. Hot again, like earlier, and like many other nights of recent. But, my temperature was of no concern because I was more troubled about the noise. Random sounds seem to be happening much more frequently. It feels like things are moving around in my place but I can't see what the cause is. It seems so weird, and now, curiously irritating. I've got to investigate, of course. I won't sleep until I check it out and find out what's going on.

I turn the lights on. Then, check the closet. All is well. I look around. No rodents, nothing's moved, nothing's out-of-place. I stand quietly and listen. Nothing. I think to myself, are there spirits? Like my imagined childhood phantoms? Gawd, how silly. I'm way too old to think like that now. How can childhood ideas like that permeate into adulthood? But, now I'm awake again and don't want to repeat a groggy "next" day by staying awake over nothing. What am I to do? There's nothing to find, nothing to fix.

Well, what the hell, let's do what works. It's time for a "demon sweep," just like the old days. I decide to be more efficient in my sweep, after all, I'm older and wiser now, so I go grab a long metal soup spoon that's in the kitchen to extend my reach. This will help. I'll be done faster, and it's sort of a mini weapon if I need it. Ha! It seems so funny. But, I just want to get my ritual done and get back to bed, and the sooner the better.

I start back in the bedroom, arms outstretched with spoon handle gripped firmly with one hand, and begin walking. Wow, I'm sweeping baddies out of my room, "Hah," I laugh to myself, how juvenile. "Make sure to get all the corners." I chuckle to myself. The bedroom will be a fast, easy sweep, I'm sure. Or, at least I am more confident in my sweeping powers now that I'm older.

"Haha," I chuckle to myself again. The absurdity. I can't believe I'm doing this. Now, what's my route? The hall, then into the kitchen, then to the dining area. Last, I'll head through the living room, then, and with a final sweep, out the front door. OK, Bedroom's done. Hallway, bathroom, now the kitchen. I begin my kitchen sweep in the back corner. While walking through the kitchen, I look out towards the living room to decide the best route in there next. Right away, I feel a strong resistance to my hand/spoon arm at the moment I'm in the middle of the kitchen. What is it? What the heck is that?

Whoa! I'm hitting something! I don't want to wipe down a cookie jar or knock-off an errant glass, or, heaven forbid, a vodka bottle off the shelf by accident. Shit! Be careful, I'm about to break something. I quickly stop to look at my spoon arm to see what it's hung upon. I'm hoping to avoid a minor kitchen incident. Then, as immediately as I had felt resistance and even before I looked, the pressure released. My arm and handle whipped forward and I whacked the refrigerator with the spoon.

The resistance had disappeared. I looked around but there was nothing, nothing that stopped the spoon. The spoon had been mid-air, not near anything. Nothing touching it, and nothing was knocked down. Well, that's a relief. Maybe I'm super tired or just having a groggy, way past midnight beer/mind fart or muscle spasm. So odd, I was sure the spoon was hung on something, but it wasn't. I did feel something though, something had grabbed my spoon. This is so curious.

I stopped for a minute for a quick thought. I couldn't immediately figure out what stopped the spoon, so I decided to continue my sweep. For me, the way my mind works, I'll do a quick mental assessment and if the answer isn't immediately available I'll stop thinking about it. However, in the background, my mind will continue to think until eventually "bing!" out of the blue comes the answer. It'll just pop in my head.

I could be doing anything. Driving the car, checking the mail, but it will come. The explanation will work it's way up, seemly on its own. I'll have figured it out. But, for this night/early morning, I'll ignore it. The feeling of something there, but not there. I'll trust it'll work in my mind in the background like a tea-pot coming to boil. Right now, I'm tired. I just want to get my "demon" sweep done and get back to sleep.

I finished the living room and with a final swoosh of my arms and spoon, exterminate the baddies out the front door. I pause in the doorway and breath in the fresh cool night air and relax. My demon sweep is done. As soon as the night chill starts to be felt, I close the door and head back to bed. Sure, I'm feeling a lit-tle foolish, but I'm also thinking that my old ritual did indeed work. I was sleepy. Maybe my ritual uses up any excess energy that's keeping me awake. But whatever the reason, the restless feeling was gone. And the fresh air felt cleansing too. I went back to bed, and sleep did come fast.

CHAPTER 2

Dreams

Sleep is what you try to find when you bed down at night. Like a romantic interest, it can be an interesting bed partner. Relaxing and satisfying, fantastic and energizing, or short and disappointing, only you know if you're not getting enough. Reminds me of the joke, "How are air, sleep, and sex all alike? Neither one matters much unless you're not getting any." Nothing much outwardly shows. If you don't get enough, you may turn any shade of grumpy. Short and disinterested towards other people, not for any viable reason. You're might be angry. Again, not for anything that really matters but only because your brain is not happy.

Your sleep deprivation has your brain complaining, "How dare you NOT let me organize, repair, post-process, and cogitate. ME, your brain, I have things that need to be done and it takes time. So because I'm not caught up on my maintenance, YOU will suffer. And maybe, as you suffer, you will realize that you need to take time to take care of me. You should know you need (I need) sleep. So until you take that time, life is going to be a bitch. I'll make you mad, help you forget, let you drive poorly, make you take instant naps, or fall asleep whenever. So keep it up and we'll see how bad it gets."

However, an interesting side note is, if you get too much sleep, you crave even more. It's an odd effect, isn't it? Not logical. But, get just the right amount and everything is right with the world. For me, I usually have no trouble getting to sleep since I've taken on my nightly beer/booze ritual. But usually, it's my dreams that get in the way. Not that I wake up in cold sweats every single night but, it's fairly often.

It is, as of late, and with increasing regularity, that my dreams are getting in the way of a restful night's sleep. They wake me up and keep me drowsy during the day. They're not just random dreams, but, usually a particular kind of dream. Interestingly enough, not one dream in particular but centered around a dream subject: floating.

Since as early as I can remember when I dream, I've often dreamed of floating. All manner of floating and each dream can be different. In one dream, I would feel weightless. That's it. No sensation, no frame of reference. I'd lose sensation in my body, my body would be weightless, lost in space. Another night I'd feel like the room would be vibrating or spinning. In yet another dream, I could float or fly like riding a roller coaster through the air. Smooth, curvy, scary, exciting, and fun. Weaving through the tops of the trees and over rooftops. Often I'd dream could float through the house like a snake on an invisible track. I'd have the feeling of being on a flowing water flume. And for some unknown reason, when I dream floated, I'd always be floating horizontally, face down, like riding a skateboard on my stomach. I guess maybe it was so I could see the ground.

In the dreams where I could float rooftop high or sail through the trees, there would always be in the back of my mind the thought, "Don't fall, you'll get hurt." A palatable touch of fear. I know I am afraid of heights and the fear of heights would often be the spark that would ignite the floating dream into a falling nightmare. And there were some dreams I could remember why I woke up, in others not. But a falling nightmare would always wake me, feeling sweaty and disoriented.

I think I've always been afraid of heights. Many people are. I believe it's the fear of not having control. When you fall, after all, you're out of control. And the results usually aren't good. In my case, I'm pretty sure my fear of heights started on a sunny fall vacation trip with my parents when I was a child. It may be one of my earliest memories. Mom, Dad, me and my younger sister, and baby Dee were at a park or some attraction in the mountains. I can't recall where, as I was so young. But I remember there were lots of steep hills and we were all there, our family, in the parking lot of whatever tourist place it was.

Then, Dad in all his misaligned wisdom thought it would be fun to swing his oldest toddler out over the rock retaining wall that the parking lot was built on. This was the mountains, and the parking lot was constructed on the side of a steep hill. There were tops of tall trees that came up level to the parking area. The ground sloped sharply down and away at the bottom. I remember while being swung in my father's arms, seeing the outside of that stone wall and then that large drop off over which he swung me over. It was a long way down to the ground. He swung me several times out over that wall. "Wheeee!" he cackled. He was laughing and grinning profusely. I was terrified. I protested loudly, screamed my displeasure. Wow, it seemed like a long way down. What if he let go, lost his grip? I still recollect the fear, "Dad, this is NOT fun! Put me down." It was all fun in his eyes, to be sure, but the damage to me was done. In my toddler mind, the distance down was horrifying. I was scared and had no control. Falling was forever going to be something I would fear.

So, in these floating dreams, I often felt nervous and afraid. It was, for sure, my fear of heights coming back to haunt me. And in most of my dreams, it seemed to take great effort to keep myself up in the air. Weird to think that something inside a dream requires so much effort, but it felt just like work. Eventually, while dream flying I would start feeling scared and nervous. And, in due course, the nervousness and the fear of falling would be the trigger that interrupted my effort. Then, the thoughts that kept me floating would stop, I'd fall.

"Oh Nooo!" I'd think. "I'm falling!" And, I'd be startled awake, heart racing panicked, and sweating.

In some other dreams, it wasn't as frightful. Instead of my body floating, I'd try to float an object using my mind. I think "levitating" an object is a better word. I'd dream of impressing my friends and family with feats or tricks of fabulous floating magic. I'd try to stand spoons on end or move forks over a table. Or stand a chair up on two legs, all by force of will. These were good dreams, usually. In them, I was popular at that moment. The envy of all. That is, when it worked, they were proud little satisfying dream successes.

In my dreams, my levitating would be difficult to do. It would seem to take great effort. I'd be lucky in those dreams if I could float while my friends or other people were watching. And, I'd want them to see me do it, like a showoff. And then sometimes, try as I might, I'd have no success. I'd look like a fool. When it didn't work, which was just as often as when it did, the dreams were frustrating and disappointing and I'd wake in the morning with the feeling of impending doom or that I had already failed the day. In either event, upon waking there was always that instant reality. The world
is heavy.

Often, I'd go to bed at night wondering about the impending morning and would frequently dread what kind of night I'd have. If it was a nightmare night? I knew I would be tired and most likely wet from sweat. I'd want to stay in bed to get more rest. "Please please, time, slow down." I'd lament. "Just another hour of sleep." I would be apprehensive that it would turn out to be another exhausting morning dragging on into an exhausting day. But up I'd get, as there were duties to perform. I'll have to catch up on sleep at a later time. Hopefully, tonight! I'm sure everybody has their nights and mornings like this. But for me, lately, waking at night seemed to be getting much too frequent.

CHAPTER 3

And Girls

I need a girlfriend. Ok, "need" is too strong a word. I want, that is, desire, a girlfriend. I haven't been in a serious relationship in quite some time. I'm sure it's a natural inclination for nearly every guy. And, it's not like I've never had a girlfriend before, but the ones that I've chosen (or let choose me) seem to have been because I've allowed myself to settle with, simply because she walks and talks and has a vagina. I guess you could say I haven't been the most successful with relationships. I mean, there was that nice Jewish girl that I had my first romantic interest with. Everybody has that one, "The Firstie." The one where you are both so young, so naive, so entranced in the newness of every-thing.

It's the wonderful, giggly-googly-eyed romance of first new love. You are mesmerized in the idea that someone other than a family member loves you. It's new ground. It's exploration. It's a transition from "me" to "us," at least for a while and you don't realize it at the time, but, it's like, "anything goes." There is no road map. The exploration of bodies and conversations with the member of the opposite sex is exciting and fresh. There is no prior history to compare it to. No expectations. No idea of the disappointing, heart-wrenching separation that is yet to come. If your lucky, the ownership of this other person's admiration lasts for months and months before the newness starts to wear off. It's wonderful. But, as is the case nearly 100% of the time, the "Firstie" relationship is eventually doomed to fail.

For one reason or another, it's not meant to last. Maybe it's a desire to experience it all over again, that newness. Relive that massive rush that fills the brain with happiness chemicals. It's not easy to get that fix with the same well-known partner. Or, perhaps it's the lure of the unknown. "What is another person like? Can it be better?" Or, very likely, it is because of the blinders that we put on from the beginning. Shades that allow us to let someone in our hearts and bodies that we weren't compatible with, not in the long run.

But all is not wasted. At least we have that experience, that memory, of the "first one." I, on random occasions, visit those thoughts. There is still a fondness there, even gratitude, when I think back to those days and her. It was exciting, it was jubilant, it was a learning experience, it was fun! How I do wish I could experience all that all over again.

Now, after her, there were of course others. Most were quick foray's into short-lived relationships, probably because I was just happy to be hanging out with a girl, any girl. But, one or more were destined to turn into long and medium-term disasters. But those stories are too long and to aggravating to relive and tell. Suffice to explain that after my last aggravating relationship, I was rather put-off with the idea of letting a new person into my life. I wasn't going to let a bad situation like that happen again. I was tired of letting just any girl in my life and trying to make it work. There has to be a better way. What I needed to learn was how to find a partner that I was attracted to, and compatible with. Someone who I'd enjoy having in my life.

Men, as a whole, do most things wrong when it comes to attracting women. Things like low confidence, talking about themselves too much, or coming across as being needy. And men, that is, most men, for the most part, are naturally intimidated by women. I am no exception. There are many reasons for this intimidation. The reasons are ingrained and deep-rooted and stem back centuries to the earliest of tribal societies. It's been ingrained over countless years. The King or tribal leader has the pick of the women. And the women understand that the leader will have the most resources to offer that will provide the best chance of her offspring to survive. Woe is it, to the low ranking male, who gets caught trying to approach a female that has the eye of the dominant or higher-ranking male. He could be cast out, killed, or be subjected to any number of tortures. And thus, these behaviors are now intrinsic. This history is why men have deep-rooted and valid reasons for having huge apprehensions when approaching a woman.

In my search for dating enlightenment, I had a grand awakening into those reasons which were brought to light in a book that I stumbled upon by pure chance. While I was randomly clicking on whatever web link that promised the lure of how to meet attractive women and get them to remove their panties, I noticed that many made references to a book called, "The Game - Infiltrating the Secret Society of Pickup Artists."

Now first, let me give credit where credit is due, definitely, and gratefully due. Neil Strauss is the author of this book. Thank you, Neil! Up until I read this book, my spinning carousel of disappointing relationships, and the unknown number of missed relationships and missed sexual opportunities were epic. All my life I'd been trying all the usual techniques. Bars, clubs, internet dating... and getting results like an average "AFC." (Average Frustrated Chump.) I didn't know what I was doing, or more likely, what I was doing wrong.

This book, "The Game," is unassuming in the title and could just as easily be dismissed as most likely uninteresting, except to perhaps to the general demographic of lustful teenage boys wanting to score any kind of girl action. Or, any fellas who would do or read anything to get close to some woman parts. I would have passed on it myself, but this book had numerous glowing reviews from many other guys. There were web pages full of once frustrated chaps who claimed that this writer brought them from the depths of woman-less, dateless despair to unimaginable abundance and successes in obtaining and attracting women.

"OK, so like everything on the internet is true. Right? And what, this link? Not a self-promoting click-bait ad? Fake book reviews maybe? Probably, and most likely marginally effective if not downright unbelievable. But maybe, it's "for real?" OK, I'll give it a read. I'll bite.

I downloaded the book and began to read. It was not captivating at first, but interesting enough to keep on reading. The first chapter is about a misfit who somehow seems to hold the key to what guys are looking for, the magic of magic's, the big reveal, the Holy Grail of dating obtained - Women beyond fantasy! The main character in the book appears to be wildly successful and it further explains his methods of how to seduce women. It then started to become fascinating.

Eventually, it tells the story about the enlightenment and transformation of a miserable guy who was a loser with women (who just happens to be the author) who turns himself into a lothario of girl attracting, confident, women seducing, dating mega-god. And he touched on many of the different techniques that some pick-up guru's focus on. At one point on social media, he became hailed as America's #1 pickup artist.

As I read through the book, I took note of the instances of discovery in what women found attractive in men. Numerous chapters were explained what is attractive to women as well as why women respond to what they respond to. To his intelligence and credit, this writer took the best attraction theories and techniques of several pickup artists and condensed the high points into a learn-able formula. A crutch for the lame to meet women. A bible for turning a man's spine into a self straightening backbone made of hardened chic magnet metal.

As I read through to the final chapters, all this knowledge congealed into a kind of life plan. I realized that, once you have the woman of your dreams, then you're ready to further the other successes in your life. After all, once the fear of women is overcome, conquering the rest of the world is easy.

The book made sense. And, all the various theories melded into a sensible formula. I was excited. Very excited! I was determined to apply all the techniques I had read and tried to fit them to me. Now, I was ready to practice on how to get the girl of my dreams. I decided I wanted a HB 8+ (In the pickup artist world, the scale is 1 - 10, with HB meaning - hot babe) and with a personality to match. I began to practice and prepare.

Using the book as my guide, it was time to give myself a makeover.

One of the ideas that make for female attraction, is the need to display as much "higher value" (DHV = demonstration of higher value) as possible. And there are several ways to do that. First, look like a million bucks. Well, at least try to be as physically attractive as possible. I starting hitting the gym, even though my job keeps me pretty trim and fit, I wanted to widen my shoulders and pump up some sexy biceps. I got a good hairstyle and started looking through fashion magazines to see what well-dressed men wear. (I would eventually come to learn that women are incredibly in-tune with fashion and notice everything a guy wears. It's something guys rarely do that women are highly in-tune with.) Those are simple if pedantic first set of rules - Look as good as you can.

Next, you will need
to DHV more than the other guy. This is done by showing women you're more valuable and/or more interesting to them than the next guy (who's probably just another AFC - Average Frustrated Chump.) You need to have good posture. Walk tall,

and have a confident attitude. That, with the sharp clothes, a constant smile and being capable of easy conversation are all a part of projecting high value. And one of the best and most effective ways to DHV is by being entertaining. Singing, playing music, performing magic, just about any talent is good. This is THE secret weapon in the seduction world. For example, just think of all the star crazed girls at rock concerts. Even the least attractive lead singer can pull in the women.

However, magic, especially magic, seems to be the biggest draw. Any magic, street magic, bar magic, even silly magic is one of the best ways to interest a girl. Like a bee being drawn to the most attractive man flower, it draws attention, makes you seem important, adds mystery, creates laughter and is a wedge to open the door into a girl's heart... and skirt. So towards that end, I decided that I needed to learn a few magic tricks. One was a bar trick where you challenge someone to stand a salt shaker on edge without it falling over. Another was a number (mind trick) guessing game, then a floating beer bottle trick. And for my grand illusion - the levitating bottle cap. Yes, a levitating bottle cap.

I knew that with magic, floating anything is mesmerizing and super impressive. It's always sure to be a crowd-pleaser.

While on another internet search, I was looking for easy magic tricks to learn, when I stumbled across a "levitating bottle cap" trick. I was amazed by the video. The trick was fabulous! I just had to learn it. It impressed me and it would certainly "Wow" other people. It was pure "inside the magician's curtain" illusion stuff. So, I spent a whopping $25 and hoped it wasn't an online rip-off.

It turned out it wasn't. It was incredibly simple. It probably cost, maybe a $1.70 worth of materials to the marketer including the DVD and DVD box and a couple of simple materials, but the information and technique were worth a fortune to me, and hopefully tons of phone numbers and removed panties. Well, at least some phone numbers and some dates. I did, after all, want to attract a high-quality gal and do the things that would keep her interested. So, with materials in hand, I practiced.

The magic was cool. I was getting cooler.

CHAPTER 4

The Daily Routine

I own and operate a property maintenance company. Not exactly what many people think like a dream job but it makes the money that pays the bills. More money than you might think. A service route of approximately 20 properties a day at an average 50 dollars per property, minus some expenses and payroll for a couple of laborers, and you can see how there's money to be made. And, I'm the boss, owner, proprietor, master of my domain. That's the best part of all. There is no judgment or oversight of middle and upper management. Nobody to report to and as flexible a schedule as I can manage. Work, no work. If I need a day off, I don't feel guilty. I send the crew off with a daily schedule and expect them to get the job done. I like to tell them that they are self-employed. I may be the one to pay them, but it's their performance that keeps the clients happy and them employed. They're not being forced to work for me or the client. But the client pays us all, so in effect, they're paying themselves. However, I do prefer to be at every job site most every visit because I want to make sure everything is done right. I want the work to be right.

Usually, after a long day at work, it's off to shower and a beer and maybe some computer or TV time to relax or finish up some paperwork. If it was a particularly hard day, (or if the sleep/dream night before was a bad one,) I'd take a much-needed snooze. Then, I'd get up and feed my pets. I'd feed myself, then call up some buddies to see who's up for some nightclub "sarging." Sarging, in pickup artist lingo, is a term for talking to people, usually girls, in clubs and bars.

I've always been comfortable by myself in clubs but a good wing-man can be a great asset. Women are everywhere but I, in the past, always relied on the crutch of music and alcohol to help me mingle. And, as a plus, at least I like to dance. And, while I'm dancing, it allows me to interact with girls. If I was lucky, the dance floor would be crowded and maybe I'd get closer to a gal than what her ordinary comfort zone would normally allow, maybe I'd even get to put my arm around my dance partner.

And, I'm a fairly good dancer too, so I've been told. Most women appreciate a guy that will even approach a dance floor. But for me, that's not a problem. The problem for me is boredom.

However, a good wing-man will give you someone to talk to while not dancing and offer encouragement. And sometimes, even a well-deserved decision check or kick-in-the-butt. For example, like when it's closing time and you're just about to stumble out the door with the grandma with false teeth and a wig and aren't thinking on how ugly the next morning is going to be.

However, In my case, and most importantly, he'll help keep me interested, motivated to stay, and not leave the club when the night hits a slow point. A moment's boredom is death to me and I tend to get the hell out of Dodge before anything interesting has a chance to happen.

My main wing-man and best friend is Mike. Mike is also my go-to buddy and my confidant. He is a good looking guy, arguably, in my opinion, better looking than me. He's a little older by a year or two and has a somewhat George Clooney look and demeanor. Plus, he works out all the time. So he sports some pretty good-sized rock-hard, bubbly arms and a full chest. I, however, have been told that I have a more of a Daniel Craig look. And that's ok as I'll take a James Bond comparison any day of the week!

It amazes me he's not fantastic with women with his "handsome-guy" build, but he is as unsuccessful as many other "AFC" guys. He seems to meet them, date them, then lose them just as quickly. And although he is my rock-solid reliable friend and wing-man, when it comes to the ladies he, unfortunately, has very little skill. However, I think with some practice and coaching, and with the things I've been learning, I'm pretty sure he could be incredible.

Mike and I first met in a Junior Chamber of Commerce meeting some years back. I joined the group because I was in a new city, knew only my sister who had moved there before me and needed some friends. Junior Chambers are great for that. They are in almost every town or city you can go to. If you're new to a place, it can be a great way to start integrating and making contacts. And, they are involved in some pretty good charity work as well. Mike and I, being of relatively close age, and with similar likes and both single, it was no wonder we became fast friends.

For Mike and me, most weekends were the same. Friday happy hour at the newest, or most popular watering hole, or, we'd go to our regular favorite Irish bar close to home. On Saturday nights we'd hit a dance club. Occasionally hanging with several other Junior Chamber friends.

I was excited to share with Mike about this tell-all book on how to meet women but I could tell he wasn't all that interested. That kind of dumbfounded me. Who wouldn't appreciate help? Especially help in attracting women? Unbelievable! Later on, though, his interest in what I had learned would eventually change, but just not yet.

After several weeks of the usual dudes-going-out routine, things started to change for me. I had been studying the book and practicing my "game." Now when we went out, we were starting to have more fun. Which translates to - meeting more girls. My self-confidence was growing exponentially along with my enthusiasm and energy level. All of the sudden we were meeting more girls than we'd ever met before. I was getting numbers and even some kisses nearly every night. They may have not been the girl of my dreams, but it was great practice for when I did come across the right one. I had several first dates and even a couple of flakes with these girls, but no one, in particular, had clicked.

Now, when Mike and I went out, it was glorious. I was learning how to be attractive. My confidence, flowing conversation, and being interesting and entertaining was working. And, Mike was beginning to notice too. I kept encouraging him to read this "pickup artist" book. I explained to him, "It's a life guide too," But, he was a slow adapter.

Unfortunately, not all nights out were successful. Some were sadly disappointing. This one evening Mike and I got dressed up to go out. Me, with a very trendy set of new clothes, Blue thin slacks, a button-down collared plaid dress shirt with Brown Chukka boots, and a belt to match. And a slim-cut light blue blazer to complete the ensemble. Mike chose to wear an old dark business suit and tie. It was classy but boring. I think he wanted to look wealthy but to me, it came across as stodgy. I suggested, actually, I made him wear a bright patterned handkerchief in his pocket so he could at least "peacock" a little. Peacocking would hopefully give gals a way to break the ice and say something to him if they wanted to, like, "I like your handkerchief." And, it DID work.

One night, Mike and I went to a newly opened restaurant bar. As we walked in, the place was packed. We had visited this restaurant bar only once before and it had a couple of unique signature drinks that we liked. Mike and I were pounding down "Cucumber Gimlet's" and nearly every chick in the place was drinking a bubbling, foggy, black-purple drink called "Berry's and Bubbles." I think they put bits of dry ice in it to get the bubbling effect. With a laugh, we called it "chic crack juice." It was highly amusing if not curious to see about every gal in the place drinking the same thing.

Once inside, I began practicing as many of the attraction techniques as I could remember. We started the evening by standing near the piano player which was located close to the entrance. This spot was central and visible to everyone. Whoever would casually look over at the piano player, would by default, see us. It was a strategic place to scope out the crowd as well as let all the women notice us. It turned out to be a great spot as this cute gal that was sitting at a 4 set (a table of 4 women) came over and opened us! ME and Mike! She just asked a dumb question, "Are you guys musicians?" It turned out that she was pretty much was just trying to impress her friends and not trying to pick us up. However, this was great for Mike and me as it was instant validation to all the other gals in the joint. If girls were coming on to us, then we were acceptable.

After a while of making our entrance known by the piano, Mike and I wanted seats and were fortunate enough to find some at the center of the main bar. We set up our "personal space" by sitting directly in the middle and spreading out to take as much room as possible without actually elbowing nearby patrons. There were several "sets" of women at tables all around, as well as at the bar, but we ignored them. I knew better than to make the impression that we were like all the other guys. Guys that would scan the crowd like sharks waiting to pounce. We made jokes with the bartenders and made a great display of laughing and acting like dominant "alpha" males. First, on our agenda, we downed a couple more stiff cocktails, those Cucumber Gimlets in their classy martini glasses.

Then, we ordered "Coffee." At this high-end bar, ordering coffee was more of an event than just "coffee." They brought out a silver platter with silver coffee pots, sugar tipped swizzle sticks, and a silver creamer ladle. At that point everyone within eye-

THE FLIGHT OF THE MAGICIAN

sight, they holding their martinis, beers, mixed drinks, and that girly bubbly vapor drink, were talking and drinking, but, they were watching us. Watching us have our "coffee." We were having a blast, and getting noticed. It had the intended effect of representing us as high-value males. This, besides just having plain old fun, is a part of the "strategy."

The women were intrigued. Who comes to a bar to drink coffee? We could feel them glancing in our direction. Mike and I talked between ourselves about who we'd like to meet but hadn't made any moves towards any women yet. About this time, a pair of gals came in and took seats at the far end of the bar. Naturally, they ordered the same bubbly purple drink that all the other girls were drinking.

These girls immediately caught my eye. Cute! A long-haired sandy blond, who I thought was just the right height with a sexy mini skirt and her friend. Who was a shorter redhead, but dressed in nearly the same outfit. Beautiful, not knockout gorgeous, but both had great figures. The blond, in my mind, was fabulous. She seemed to possess all that I wanted, at least visually, in a girl. Mike noticed too, because I told him to look, so we agreed. These became our targets. They were hotties!

We were still making a point of laughing and having fun when I saw one of our targets take out her phone to photograph their freshly made bubbly drinks. "Opportunity!" I thought." I didn't want Mike messing up our chances with these two, so I told him to go "open" a 6 set table of girls near us by asking them the question. "Who lies more, men or women?" Hesitant, but compliant, off he went. With a question like that, he was sure to draw up some conversation.

Meanwhile, I dashed down to the end of the bar and offered to take their picture with their drinks. "I'll take your picture with your drinks." I offered. They of course agreed, and, that was my "in." The taller blond and I immediately started a conversation.

I was relieved to find her lively and personable. After being girl-friend-less for so long I found her and charming and open manner a lonely man's dream come true.

After the usual banter of home, work, and family, I decided to practice a few of my new pickup artist techniques. I commented on how "embarrassingly short her skirt was and how she shouldn't be seen in public wearing that." I then immediately followed with "how hot and attractive it was on her." (That I had learned was a push-pull comment.) Then, I continued to flirt by saying, "If you're not careful, it would be far too easy for a guy to get his hand lost in there." This was meant to allude to sex, without actually mentioning sex. Getting a girl thinking about sex is far better than talking about sex. It gets her mind working in that direction. If you mention sex directly to a gal, you're at risk of her setting her off, even getting her defensive. That is... she may go into "anti-slut" mode. No girl wants to admit that they are easy, even though the consensuses is, is that women are just as horny as men, maybe even more.

Mike returned and joined me and the girls after talking to the table of six. He did make some good conversation with the table of 6 women, and his tie did get noticed. I imagined he eventually ran out of things to say because he came back to the bar in a relatively short amount of time. But it was ok because I had already made my "in." We were safe to talk to.

After introducing Mike and after a good half-hour of small talk, we fond out that the blonde, Lisa, and the redhead, Christy, were just about ready to set off to hit another bar. I could tell Lisa was started getting upset with Christy because she was the one wanting to leave. I could tell Lisa was happy that she and I were hitting it off and she didn't want to leave. Then, we found out that they were sisters. Really? Surprise. I hadn't even thought that they looked all that similar. And, then we found out that they drove together. Damn. And, to top it off, Christy wasn't digging Mike at all. I think she thought he was too old for her. And

THE FLIGHT OF THE MAGICIAN

his suit didn't help him at all as it made him look even older than he was.

I decided to hit the bathroom before they left fully intending to come back and find them at the bar. I was looking forward to asking them where they were going so we could continue the night, and I'd get the opportunity to get to know Lisa even better.

Unfortunately, that didn't happen. I didn't get the chance. I returned only to find that they weren't at the bar. Oh no! I missed a dream girl! I couldn't believe that they had left. Maybe they thought I had left first. Now they were gone! I asked Mike where they were, "Did they say where they were going?" He didn't know. All he could say was that they had gone. I ran out the front door after them hoping to catch them in the parking lot. No sign of them. All I did see was a car leaving the parking lot that I assumed was theirs, but it was too late. I was NOT happy. The restaurant bar was about to close for the night and the rest of the evening was uneventful. It was a fun evening to be sure, but the loss of that chance of connecting with that hottie stung in my mind for a long time.

Many weeks later I was going through my phone and found a number I didn't recognize. Then it hit me like a lightning strike, "Oh no, Damn it all! It was that hottie, Lisa!" I had "number closed" her and didn't even remember getting it. Was I THAT buzzed? Wow, that's super frustrating!

I figured that far too much time had passed to give her a call. I'm sure she would have thought "Who? Where?" or maybe it might have seemed a bit disrespectful on my part since I hadn't called her at all, as it had been too long and our meeting too short. I made a mental note to myself right then, "Don't drink too much when going out." Opportunities can be lost.

CHAPTER 5

Bar Tricks

Our usual Friday night routine was to hit our regular happy hour hangout where everybody in town would go to see and be seen. Then Saturday nights were off to one of two places that had a dance floor and no cover. Due to my recently acquired knowledge of the pickup arts, I had gotten pretty good at "opening," that is meeting girls, and in demonstrating higher value (DHV.) I would start with a few simple magic tricks that would bring in some laughs, some groans, or even win us some drinks. It was a fabulous way to appear interesting and fun to girls but to mostly helped stand out from the crowd. We also frequented only a few bars as the book recommended that it's beneficial to get familiar with the bouncers, doormen, DJ's, and even owners.

It was our aim when we walked in, to have the staff "high five" us or shake our hands or at least acknowledge us with a nod or wave. That would show clout to any girls around as well as make us seem important. We also felt like this was "our house." We were comfortable there. That gave us even more courage. Even though the girls didn't know us, they could see that we were somewhat important and that made them more interested in that we had social standing. And that was a big subconscious plus, on both sides, when approaching females.

Eventually, our weekends had gotten so regular that most of the bartenders and bouncers did know us by name. And, they also knew what we were after, meeting girls. But, then, wasn't every guy there after the same thing?

One particular evening Mike and I were accompanied by my sister, her best friend, and my brother-in-law's sister who was visiting for the weekend. In the past, my sister had even dated Mike for a short while, but she had gotten tired of him quickly. Turned out he wasn't as ambitious as she liked. He also performed many of the same "AFC" (Average Frustrated Chump) mistakes most guys make with girls. Eventually, those mistakes add up and the girl becomes disinterested. Mike had great schooling, interesting past jobs, a decent job, well-traveled, and he was good looking! But, regardless of his glowing attributes, he didn't know how to keep her attraction up. She noted to me that he seemed to be afraid of success, despite having many great ideas and all kinds of different talents. He got boring.

We were all in the club and the girls had gone dancing on the dance floor. Mike and I watched and talked and sipped our drinks. Having girls with us already made Mike and I look "acceptable." Other gals in the place didn't have any idea that they were mostly my relatives. To the other women, guys with girls hanging with them were all they saw, and that alone established our acceptability. As a side note, a normal guy who wants to meet girls, and who doesn't know any better, would probably think it wasn't in his best interest to be out with other girls that he's not romantically interested in. In actuality, the reverse is true. Hanging out with girls increases your chance of meeting more women. It sounds counter-intuitive, but it's true, and it works.

At one point, Mike and I decided to get a fresh round of drinks. When I turned around towards the bar I spied two cute girls sitting directly across from us. I decided that instead of ordering from our side of the bar, we'd wiggled up to their side (as it was fairly crowded) to order our drinks. Then, we'd be so close they would have no choice but to notice us. Once there, I started an opening routine.

Me: Hi there!
Them: Hello
Me: "You girls come here to dance?
One says "yes," the other says, "no." One, has a smile, the other, a raised eyebrow.
Me: You look like smart girls, let me get your opinion on something
Them: OK, what?

(Here is where I mention, before headed out for the evening, as I am getting ready, I spray two different colognes on each of my wrists. In a minute you'll see why.)

I position myself between them with my back against the bar so they're less distracted by other people and more focused on me. Then, I hold out one wrist to each girl, in turn.

I say, "Here smell my wrist. I've been sampling new colognes. Tell me which one you like better."
Them, "Oh, OK." They comply.
Me, "Now smell the other. There's a reason why I want you to help me."

(They each pick their favorite)

During this exercise, this allows me to get close to them and get some "kino." "Kino" is a pickup lingo term for light touching. As they smell my wrists, I touch their shoulder, or their arm, and lean into them. This "Kino" helps assure them I'm "safe." My touch, unconscious to them, helps them feel more comfortable towards me.

I start my story with:

Me: "Ladies, the reason I'm asking you this is, I've been wearing this same cologne forever. You see, a long time ago my sister and I used to hang out and go to clubs together. Then, one night, as we're getting ready, I see her spraying on cologne. I take a look at what she's putting on and notice that it's a men's cologne. I say "SUSAN! What are you doing? That's men's cologne!" She then says, "Yeah, I know. But, I like the scent of it so much that I love to wear it." So me, being a smart guy, I think to myself, "Well, if my sister, a female, likes this men's cologne so much that she wears it, then that's what I need to be wearing." So, I've been wearing it ever since. And, that's been years ago."

Them: They both laugh.

Me: "But now I've been thinking I need something different, something newer, or better, so I'm trying out these new co- lognes. Which did you say you like the better?"

So now I'm in. The story worked and it seems that they're be- coming more comfortable with me. I ask their names and ex- plain that it's a true story, which it was. These girls are Cindy and Lori. Cindy is tall, (taller than most girls) but she has a super thick head of hair which makes her seem taller than she is. It's was the kind of hair that you'd wonder if you tried to run your fingers through it if it was going to be hard to get them out. Kind of like a super curly, light brown highlighted lions mane. Lori, on the other hand, had straight red hair and was shorter, but she also had a great figure just like Cindy. The downside for me was Lori smoked. Not that it's always a deal-breaker for me, but, see- ing that Cindy was just as cute, thin, and sexy and didn't smoke. She was the one I was attracted to. Anyway, I could tell, as things began to progress, that she was digging me, even though (or maybe because) I had walked in with other girls. Or, perhaps it was because I had gotten their guard down with some "kino" and my perfume story. It was probably both. A combination of professional strategies!

I found out that Cindy and Lori were out that night because Cindy was celebrating a special occasion. She was celebrating the anniversary of her passing her nurse's exam. And, there was also a quick mention of one of them dumping a crappy boyfriend. After a short time of light banter, sipping cocktails and watching the dance floor, the girls decided that they wanted to dance. Mike and I opted to stay at the bar and as Mike and I watched them dance, it was apparent to me that Cindy definitely the sexier of the two. When she danced, all the guys watched. It was interesting to see that, when random guys tried to dance with her, she'd just ignore them and keep doing her own thing. Eventually, Lori paired up with some guy, but Cindy kept on dancing by herself on the crowded dance floor. She would often look my way to see if I was watching. And, damn straight I was! Sometimes I would nod in acknowledgment or tip my beer at her. I was holding my cool. (I didn't want to be like all the other guys watching and drooling over her, yet I probably was.)

I watched the girls dance, and was captivated. I wasn't going to let this one slip through my hands, so I decided I would pull out all my best bar tricks. When they returned from the dance floor, I introduced them to the rest of my female posse and without letting them notice, my sister secretly gave me her approval of them. I then performed my leaning salt shaker trick and bet them a beer on it. I allowed them to try it first and then, of course, I won the bet. This trick was good for some groans, rolled eyes, and, of course, a fresh beer. Having won the beer, I knew that, because Cindy went along with the trick, she was somewhat interested and had made something of an investment in me. Only a beer, but still an investment of sorts.

As the evening continued, it was obvious that Cindy was wanting more attention. Lori and Mike chatted but I was pretty sure that Mike was heading towards a DLV fail. (DLV means, demonstrate lower value.) That's done by a number of things like being awkward or trying too hard. I didn't want to interfere in their banter and because I wanted some alone time with Cindy, I stole Cindy away to a far corner table on the outside patio. It was as secluded and quiet a place as I could find. I then performed "The

Cube" exercise on her. "The Cube" is a personality quiz of sorts and is a reasonably good way to determine someone's current state of mind and hopefully reveal some of their personality. It's also a great way to build trust, create interest, and start a bond, and possibly get even more "kino." I had performed it several times on other girls with good results. I could pretty much tell which ones had problems in their lives, had low self-esteem, or some other issue, etc. It was a fun and strangely accurate game. And girls seemed to love it. Anything that has to do with personality quizzes is another form of "chick-crack" which girls love. I've never met a girl that would refuse any type of personality test.

"The Cube" is a series of questions where you ask things like, "Imagine a room, now imagine a cube in the room, imagine a horse in the room, imagine a storm, and so on." There is no "right" answer to any of the questions but the answers they give may lead insight into a way that person thinks. If they imagine a large room, then it's a good bet they live in an expanded world or are well-traveled. If they say that their cube is small and off in a corner, then you might extrapolate that they see themselves as a small part of a big world. If their horse is quiet and calm, then their ideal mate is probably quiet and reserved. If they imagine a storm that's a hurricane inside their room and wind whirling around their cube, it's almost a sure bet they have turmoil currently in their lives, it surrounds them.

The cool part of the exercise is, whatever answer your subject delivers, if you don't have an idea what it means, then all you have to do is ask, "What do you think this-and-this means to you?" They'll tell you. All you have to do is listen. You'll get a good impression, by their answers, on their state of mind. It's almost as simple as, happy people have happy thoughts. Sad people have dark thoughts. The result is, the person you're testing, afterward, feels as though they've shared themselves with you, and they have. The Cube test is probably the quickest way to form a bond to someone you've just met.

On some of the girls I've used it on, it's also been a direct indicator to steer away and out of the path of probable trouble. One girl that I took on a first date, I used The Cube to try and start that quick connection. Her answers, actually her "Storm" answer was so alarming that it gave me pause to think if I should ever ask her out again. As the date continued, my suspicions were confirmed as I came to find out she was in the middle of, not one, but a couple of court battles, ex-husband disputes, financial troubles, etc. Needless to say, as sorry as I felt for her, I didn't pursue her any further.

On the other hand, it's easy to tell when people are at ease. They'll give light-hearted, colorful, and creative answers. It'll be a fun test and you'll have established the beginnings of a personal bond. It's great for getting close to a possible romantic partner as you'll be engaged in conversation, close, and hopefully, alone. It's a good combination for something passionate to happen.

As Cindy and I were alone at that table, I moved in close and held her hands. I looked directly at her when I asked my questions and listened intently to her answers. I knew that, by my studies, if she started the "triangle" with her eyes, by looking from eye-to-eye then down at my lips, then that was an indicator that she was thinking about kissing. I saw her do that several times and I returned the indicator by doing the same. When the exam was over I ended it with my making a joke. I claimed, "It was all fake, I made it up!" Cindy laughed in response but knew it wasn't true.

She had passed all the "The Cube" test with flying colors even though it's not a pass/fail. She came across as a stable, goal-oriented person without any apparent issues in her life. Then, as we sat for a minute in the reflection of our talk, it felt as though we had just shared something. And as we sat, I could sense her attraction to me. I could tell she was intrigued and enamored.

Then, physically close to each other and somewhat by ourselves, we began to "make out."

After we "made out" for a while we returned to the bar where Mike and Lori were still talking. (I didn't want to overdo it, it's a kind of "takeaway." If you give someone a taste, then you are setting them up to keep them wanting more. A normal AFC guy would just try to make out for as long and as much as possible, hoping it would finally lead into a bedroom. That procedure rarely works. On our walk back to Mike and Lori I was thinking to myself, "That Cube test is the best thing I've ever learned. I think I may be connecting with someone that I really like! I'm glad I've done the practice to get it right."

For Mike, the fact that he was still talking with Lori was a good sign. I was kind of shocked and was hoping that he'd keep it up. However, to keep everyone interested, I did a couple more tricks for our group, the floating beer bottle. (It's where you slide your hand slowly up the bottle all the while keeping the bottle stationary in midair. Think like a vertical Michael Jackson moonwalk, but with a beer bottle.) That was good for some more eye-rolls and laughs. Then, not wanting to rely only on cheesy bar tricks, I decided to pull out my show stopper. My piece-DE-resistance. My one real and rarely performed trick - the "levitating bottle cap."

I asked my bartender friend Shawn for one of his "special" beer bottle caps. He obliged and played along. After he examined several bottles, he selecting the perfect one and tristed off the cap, then passed it over. (There is nothing special about the bottle cap, but you got to play your audience!) I let everyone hold the bottle cap to see that it wasn't rigged. I then took the cap, held it between my thumbs in front of me, then flicked, and spun it as fast as I could.

Immediately I put one hand under the now spinning, floating bottle cap and one hand "directing it" on the side. I floated the cap about 5 inches over my hand until it started to slow it's spin, almost a half a minute, then I caught it midair. Everyone and I mean EVERYONE is amazed. Clapping and astonishment abound. I told everyone it's my, "once a month" trick and refuse to do it again as it takes far to much effort. It is a true professional illusionist trick and I will not divulge how it's done. But for me, however, I DHV'd over every guy in the place, no one could match my status. And, the best thing for me was, Cindy was hooked.

CHAPTER 6

The Best Date

I had dated before. I've had had sex before. Naturally, not nearly as much or as often as I wished, and most of the time my dates ended up by breaking off early or my going home alone, or, sometimes on a particularly fortunate night, there could be a drunken "oh-my-god-it's-getting-light-out" revelation in the back seat of my car.

On this one lucky/unlucky instance, I was happily naked and sweating in the back seat of a car. In the heat of the summer, during the heat of passion, there was a bright light. And then... "tap, tap, tap" at the window. Of necessity, all the windows were up to keep out the mosquitoes. There's nothing worse than swatting mosquitoes off your bare behind while concentrating about doing-the-deed. With the windows closed, we two, hot, drunk, horny, and sweaty bodies were going at it. Car windows were so fogged that they dribbling on the inside. It was indeed a hot summer night.

As my luck with women would have it, that tap, tap, on the window was the police. The spot we thought was secluded and out of sight was viewed, by the landowner as trespassing, and he did not like strange cars driving through his fruit grove at night. It wasn't a late-night parking friendly zone. Embarrassed and highly disappointed in the interruption, we rapidly and clumsy, did a super-fast, putting on our clothes episode. During this, the police gave us a condescending interrogation while our garments were being sorted and applied. We were sternly asked to move on and we eventually went on our way feeling rather like scolded dogs who had gotten caught pooping on the living room carpet. Not the best end to a date.

Now, however, regular dating was a nice change. I had found myself a reliable and enthusiastic partner in Cindy. Over the next couple of weeks, she and I would make a point to go out at least one-night mid-week, and Mike and I integrated her and occasionally some girlfriend of hers into our weekend bar visits. Cindy and I became an item in a very short time. We hung out and talked with the bartenders and waitresses and always seemed to have a great time. Naturally, I stopped using my attraction techniques on other women, however, I would still try to help out Mike now and then. Mike had even told me that he started reading that "pickup" book I had told him about, although I doubted he had. I'd occasionally quiz him or mention a part in the book and he didn't seem to know what I was referring to. Whatever... Mike was going to be Mike. Good luck bro.

Even Cindy seemed to notice he needed some help at times. She would oftentimes get on the bandwagon and help him by picking up his conversation with a girl when it started to slack. When Mike would run out of things to say or stay on boring topics, she would chime in and help him along. But, most of the time, Cindy and I would talk between ourselves or dance together. Or, on occasion, I'd just watch her on the dance floor while she watched me watching her. Like when we first met. It seemed to be our "thing."

For Cindy and me, it wasn't long, perhaps our third or fourth date that we consummated our relationship. Our very first full night "together" was planned sex. Or more appropriately, "an evening of dinner and designed romance." It was a far cry from my past dates with the strategy of, "I hope to get some booty before the alcohol wears off." For our upcoming date, we decided to not go out, but, to stay in. Instead of heading out and drinking, dancing, and bar hopping with friends, we planned a simple and delicious dinner at home. We cooked Angus steaks, a dried tomato salad, lightly steamed green beans seasoned with Anise seed, red wine, and a movie. Simple, but yummy.

We both knew exactly what this night would lead to. We talked about it the entire week beforehand. It was a fun tease when she talked to me on the phone. "And, this weekend," She'd say, "I'll be at your house... And we'll be by ourselves... and, I'll be able to kiss you without anyone watching..." and on and on. It turned me on and I could hardly wait. The anticipation was so much a part of the fun.

The evening went exactly as planned and was perfect. I introduced her to my pets. My parrot "love machines," (they're very affectionate,) Big Red and Cancun. She acted interested in them but I could tell they made her a little nervous. If there was a low point, that may have been it. Dinner was fantastic, the movie was good, and with plenty of wine at the ready, being there at home, made everything super comfortable. This all lead up to an evening of vigorous lovemaking. It was untroubled, exhilarating, and satisfying sex. The whole evening was enjoyable. I knew I was going to sleep well that night.

Sleep well... hmm, not exactly. I tried hard to fall asleep but I just couldn't get settled. Maybe it was because I had a hot sexy girl next to me. Maybe I was afraid I'd fart too loud or she'd fart out loud and I'd have to pretend I didn't hear it, or, forbid if there was something smelly going on. I was awake and tired, fidgety, and maybe a bit nervous. It wasn't until close to 4 am after going to the kitchen and downing a full beer that I finally fell asleep.

At about 6 am she woke me up.

Her: "Matt, what are you doing?"
Me: "What?"
Her: "Are you trying to get me out of bed?"
Me: "What do you mean?"
Her: "You were pushing on me. Do you want me to get up?"

Me: "No, I am just sleeping."
Her: (somewhat relaxing) "Well, I thought you wanted me to get out of bed. It felt like you were pushing me."
Me: "No, not at all. Stay here, in bed, with me."

I pushed the hair out of her face and rubbed her shoulders as she sat on the edge of the bed. I kissed her back and shoulders, and she leaned back towards me. We had sweet morning sex.

CHAPTER 7

Things That Move

Cindy came over a second time that week. And, in the middle of the week no less. I guess I had probably done something right the first time. There can be, understandably, a concerned fear for many men that their lady love might go home unsatisfied.

I'm a pretty smart guy, not the smartest, but in my opinion a bit higher than most. I research things I'm interested in. Especially when it concerns women. And, some of that research includes being talented in bed. It's one thing to read books on meeting and attracting a woman. But then, after that, you have to know how to keep them. Besides good conversation, fun times, and respect, it's essential to know how to make their bodies happy. Guys' bodies are easy, especially when compared to women's. So, its best to know what works in the bedroom. To all the guys out there I say, "Get out your sex instruction books fellas, and your significant other will stay your significant other!"

And, although it is great to be able to attract a multitude of women, and please them., for me, "enough" means having just one. Once you've become a bonded with the one that you mentally connect with, that also looks good enough for you to desire her, then, of course, you wish to please her. Please a woman and you can be assured that your position of acting the role of the man is accomplished. If she decides to leave you, then it won't be because you've slacked in your sexual duties, it'll have to be because of something else.

I believe that it takes attention and intuition to tell when a woman is satisfied. You have to think of it like dancing. When you hear the music, you feel the rhythm, you move with your partner, and you try to anticipate the right moves as the music changes. If you get it right, then the dancing is great. It's organic and natural. If you do it wrong it can be clumsy and a fumble of moves to find the right sensation. However, if you're in tune and if you use some sexual prowess, you can get into the rhythm and make the movements to create the crescendo that you're antici-pating. Aloofness in bed is not good when it comes to making love. You can, most of the time, tell that a good dancer is pretty much good in bed. And really good dancing takes practice. I read about and try to learn the good moves and techniques about sex. Then, when the opportunity presents, I try to do it right.

Tonight, as Cindy stayed over again, I had my normal shot of al-cohol before bed. I didn't want Cindy to think I was an alcoholic so I drank it in the kitchen while she was getting ready in the bedroom. We fell asleep right after another round of passionate bedroom Olympics.

At about 2 am she woke me up.

Cindy: "Hey, did you hear that?"
Me: Groggy but awake: "No, what?"
Cindy: "There was a noise."
Me: "What noise?"
Cindy: "I think there is something in the closet."
Me: "Are you sure? It wasn't my talking alarm clock, was it? You know it does it's own thing sometimes."
Cindy: "No, it wasn't the clock. There IS something in the closet."
Me: "Ok, I'll take a look."

I got up, opened the closet doors, and saw nothing out of the or-dinary. There was, however, a box of dress shoes that had fallen to the floor. A box that I usually keep on the top shelf. I gathered up the shoes, put them back in the box and returned them to where they usually sat.

Me: "It was just a shoebox that fell. I'm not sure why, but it did."
Cindy: "Yeah, it was loud, but I've been hearing some strange sounds all night."
Me: "Really? What sounds?"
Cindy: "I don't know. It's like you have mice or something. Or, maybe it's your pet birds. I'm not really sure."
Me: "What?"
Cindy: "Off and on, I hear things clicking or shuffling. I thought it was just this old house or the pets but look over there, that picture on the desk has fallen over. I know it was standing up last night. I asked you if it was your father, remember?"

Me: "Yeah, I remember. It was standing. Maybe we had a mini earthquake or something."
Cindy: "Could be. Maybe I'll check the news in the morning. And by-the-way, you were awesome tonight."

That made me smile. We cuddled up together then went back to sleep and had no other interruptions for the rest of the night.

Now, after several sleepovers with Cindy, I noticed that I was beginning to sleep better, especially when she stayed over, although the random pattern of waking to odd noises in the house still seemed to occur. Maybe it was because there was an extra pair of ears listening when she was with me. If it wasn't her waking me having heard something, it was me. It was often enough that we started keeping a mental list of nights when we heard noises, or when things had fallen over during the night. Usually, it was small items that were out of place. We tended to believe that it was a rogue mouse, the birds, or maybe the house settling or a breeze.

Occasionally, Cindy would tell me she woke up feeling funny.

She said it felt like she was being pushed or something was moving her hair around which caused her to wake up. Most of the time we would often chalk it up to sleeping together and not being used to each other. We even toyed with the idea that the house might be haunted. After all, it was one of the older homes in the area. I had never heard any stories about it if it was haunted. That is if there were any. We both thought it was, "Silly to think there is such a thing as house ghosts." We both agreed that ghosts seemed like the least possible idea. It was one of those notions you won't allow yourself to entertain because it seems so ridiculous. But, we both knew the other was thinking about it.

CHAPTER 8

Bar Tricks and the Plus 1

For the past several weeks Cindy and I had been having a great time. Together with Mike, we continued our weekend routine. And, for Cindy and I, we had still had our midweek at home alone time. However, Cindy and I had decided to have a side goal of getting Mike a girlfriend so we could all hang as couples and not have the odd "third wheel" situation. There was, on occasion, times when Mike would even get on my nerves. Sometimes he would tend to hover. He would linger around us and chain talk about inane subjects that we had no interest in. For example, what new building was being built where and who owns it. He'd go on endless ramblings about buildings, buildings that neither he nor I or anyone we knew had anything to do with, or would ever have had anything to do with. Just a droll banter of endless "buildings" talk. I could never figure the reason why.

Eventually, I'd have to give him a nudge to get him to move on. Sometimes I'd have to say. "Mike, I think it's time to go home." Or, I'd tell him, "Cindy and I have some "business" to take care of." Therefore, whenever we were out, it was our mission to try and get Mike a date. Maybe he'd be more inclined to peel off earlier in the evening so Cindy and I could be on our own.

One night, we three were at the dance club in the company of a good lively, crowd. There were 3 sets of rowdy bachelorette parties in the place and all the bridesmaids were buzzing around the brides-to-be laughing, drinking, and acting silly. Our chairs were close to the dance floor and in a great people viewing spot near the bar where we could pretty much see almost everything going on in the club. It was great for us in that, our bartender friend would hold these spots for us if he knew we were coming in. I'd make a point of texting him if I thought we would be heading there for some fun.

After a while of sitting at our "regulars" seats, one of the bachelorette parties came up to the bar and began to order drinks right next to us. While they ordered, we all engaged in the usual "who's getting married" questions. Mike gave me the signal that he was "really" interested in one, maybe two, of the bachelorettes so I decided to perform some tricks to hold their attention for a while. This would give Mike a little more time to strike up a conversation with some of the gals in the group. First, I showed them the floating bottle trick. They all moaned and laughed as it wasn't very impressive. So, I decided to do another trick to keep them there a little while longer. Hopefully, this would give Mike his chance. I thought the "Floating Bottle Cap" trick should do it, so I started that routine.

I asked the bartender, "Can you get me one of those special bottle caps?"

He nodded and pulled out a fresh beer from the cooler. He then gave me the bottle cap off and poured the beer for me.

I began my trick by saying, "Here is a very special bottle cap. They only sell beers with this particular cap here at Johnny's."

I held up the cap then handed it to the girls.

I told them, "Take a good look and inspect that cap carefully." The girls obey. One by one they look it over.

"OK, now give me the cap. I only can do this once a month because it's so difficult." I held the cap up for all to see and then toss it back and forth between my hands while saying, "I'm going to float this cap using intense concentration and... mostly... a whole lot of luck."

They all giggled a little bit. I knew I had everybody's attention. I saw Mike explaining the trick I was about to do to one of the girls he was interested in. "Good." I thought, "He's making a move."

I positioned the cap between my thumbs, and, as quickly as I could, spun the cap with my thumbs and then immediately moved one hand under and one hand to the side. The cap spun rapidly, midair, between my cradling hands.

As soon it began to spin, I instantly realized my error. I had forgotten to set up the trick! Terribly confused, at once I thought, "Why is the trick working? And working well." The cap continued to spin and spin fast, but kind of differently. It was also rotating end over end.

I was so startled that I slapped my hands together to make it stop. I slapped so hard on the cap that it cut little dimpled spots of blood in a perfect "cap sized" circle on the palm of my hand. Oblivious to the applause and laughter, I quickly turned toward the bar and grabbed a napkin to dapple up the little ring of blood dots.

Cindy turned toward me, looked at my hand, and asked, "Are you OK?" I continued to press the napkin into my palm and then stared at the cap. I picked it up and slowly flipped it over and examined it carefully. "It's just a cap," I say to myself.

I then turned to Cindy and said, "I didn't do it." She said, "What? What do you mean you didn't do it? You did great!" I explained to her, "I didn't set up the trick." She remarked back, "What do you mean you didn't set it up?" I explained, "There's a special way to make this trick work and I didn't set it up beforehand. But, it worked anyway." Cindy looked at me with a confused expression. I said, "I think it actually floated by itself. And, I'm not sure if I even believe it." Cindy just stared at me. I think she was waiting for me to make a joke about it.

I could feel my hands begin to shake. "I'm going outside for some air." I made a quick exit out the front entrance and once outside on the sidewalk, I sat down on the curb. My hands were shaking a lot now. The one hand still had the sting of being cut with the bottle cap. I kept reexamining the cap.

Cindy joined me outside. "What's wrong?" She was worried.
Me, "I think I actually floated the bottle cap."
She asks, "Really? What do you mean?"
Me: "I'm not for sure, but, I think it really floated."
Mike came outside and joined us. "What's going on? Those bachelorettes are still in there! Let's go back in! What's wrong with him?" He said as he pointed at me.
Cindy: "He says he said he made the cap float but he said he didn't set the trick up beforehand."
Mike: "No way. That's bullshit. "
I say, "Yeah, I think I did. I haven't had very much to drink and I know I didn't set it up before it started floating."
Mike says, "Can you do it again?"
I said to Mike, "I don't know. I'm almost afraid to try."
Mike: "Well, try to do it again, see if you can."
"I say, "Yeah, OK, I'll try."

As I stood up. I could feel my heart racing and my hands were still trembling. I lined up the cap between my thumbs, flicked it for a spin, and the cap shot off and bounced down the sidewalk. I tried again, and the same thing happened. I said to them, "I don't know. My hand is throbbing from slamming the cap and my heart is racing like I just chugged 4 energy drinks. I don't think I can do it."

We decided we'd call it an early night even though Mike was disappointed about leaving the bachelorettes behind. On the way home, we all decided that I must have set up the trick but didn't remember doing it. For me, I wasn't sure of either scenario.

CHAPTER 9

The Strange Night

A few evenings later, Cindy had decided to come over and on this night, the most disturbing thing happened. We were beginning to really enjoy our at-home "dates." We made another simple yet tasty dinner with a skillet grilled steak, sirloin again, my favorite, and a fresh mixed greens salad drizzled with a homemade white balsamic vinaigrette dressing and another bottle of delicious Cabernet wine. It had been a hard workday for me and after dinner, sleep came unusually fast and easy. I didn't even take the time to down my usual shot of alcohol before bed. I was very comfortable and relaxed as we slid into bed. My belly was full and I had my soft, sexy, naked, spooning partner next to me. Immediately I fell into a deep sleep.

After what seemed like only seconds, I awoke to a shrill scream and then the sensation of feeling my head bounce up and down on the pillow. Jarred awake, I turned to see that Cindy had retreated to a far corner of my bedroom and was staring at me. She finally muttered with her fists covering her mouth, "I saw you. I saw you above your bed. I saw you floating above your bed and the covers... and, the covers were moving. Like a wave. Like a wave of water, or, on a flag."

I said drowsily, "What?" Cindy responded
with, "I had gotten up to go to the bathroom and when I came out, you were there, floating. I saw you. You were about a foot above the bed with the covers over you. And the covers were

moving. What was that, a trick? Please tell me this isn't some new trick or something, is it? I answered her somewhat groggily, "What are you talking about? Floating? I was sleeping. Are you sure you saw me floating?" She answered, "yes, I saw you floating above your bed. And when I yelled, you fell. I don't understand what just happened. It's a trick, right?"

"Cindy, I was asleep." I told her, "I was having a dream. I think I was dreaming that I was flying. I can't remember exactly what the dream was about but, I do remember feeling like I was flying." She said, "You were also talking out loud but couldn't understand what you were saying." She came over to the bed and sat down. We sat there in thought for a minute. I suggested, "Well, maybe you just heard me talking about floating or something like that while I was dreaming." She told me she was sure she saw what she saw. I then said, "You know, I've always had dreams about flying. Not every night but fairly often, and for pretty much my entire life. I thought everyone had them. I can't always remember what happens in my dreams, but when I do, they often seem to be about me flying, or floating, or moving something around. My dreams almost always end with me falling, and that's when I'll wake up. Sometimes I'll feel terrified like they were real."

Cindy asked, "So now, what are we going to do? There's definitely something creepy going on." I answered, "I don't know." She said, "We need to video this. If it happens again, I want you to see it." I said, "What are you talking about? Can we talk about this in the morning? It's still the middle of the night and we need to get some sleep." She said, "OK, but no way am I sleeping in here, in this bedroom. There's is something weird in here going on. I'm going to go sleep on the couch." I wasn't happy about that and gave her a pouty face and said, "Come on back here, come back to bed." That didn't change her mind, so I joined her in the living room.

Over breakfast the next morning we decided that we'd get a

small tripod and a motion detector camera and set it up in the bedroom. Hopefully, this would help her feel better and we'd catch something happening if something actually happens. Cindy remarked, "Maybe you've got a real house ghost in here. Or maybe you're just putting me on and tricking me with one of your special magic tricks. Either way, I want to find out." I said, "OK, it sounds like a plan." My curiosity was also on the rise. So, later that same day, I bought a camera and a tripod and set it up next to the bed.

Cindy was lucky enough to have been assigned normal hours at the hospital as she had only started working at her new position a few weeks earlier. So our schedules, at least for a while, were mostly the same. That meant it was easy for her to pack some things and stay over on any given night, so, that's what she did. For the following few mornings, when we woke up, Cindy would rush to check the video before she'd do anything else. Then, finding that nothing interesting was recorded, we'd both get ready for work. The camera worked by a motion sensor and had night vision, and nothing other than a nightly bathroom visit was seen.

One early morning, however, there was something different. We both were awakened to a loud crash. I felt a sharp pain on my lip. I had a small TV that sat on the dresser next to the bed. Now, it was on the floor dangling by its cable. Cindy immediately rushed to the camera while saying, "Oh wow! Let's check the video!" We re-wound the video to the time that it came on. The camera had picked up the TV just as it was falling off the dresser. We couldn't see what caused the TV to fall. It appeared to have just tipped over. That was it. There wasn't anything that would suggest what made the TV move. And, dammit the pain in my lip, hurts! The power plug end of the cord hit me in the face as it pulled out of the wall socket and whipped over the top of the dresser. It was a sharp pain and it left a tiny red cut right above my lip.

Then, the next night, something much more interesting happened. As I was waking up, Cindy yelled over to me, "Matt, check it out!" The tripod and camera were unplugged and leaning on a bookshelf on the far side of the room behind a chair. She said, "I've got to see this." She rushed to replay the video. As we viewed it, we saw that it turned on to record, but we couldn't see anything out of the ordinary. We saw only the foot of the bed. Then, we noticed the video slowly rotating, filming a slow pan of the room. First, it starting at the foot of the bed, then moved diagonally to the ceiling, then a slow pan around the room then down then to the bottom of the window curtains. It continued this rotating scan until it looked like it came to the end of the charging cable, and fell with a jerk. Then nothing. It had powered off, and that was the end of the recording.

OMG! Cindy yelled," That's so freaky. It looks like the room is moving. And I think, It didn't come on because something was moving, it came on because the camera itself was moving! Now, what are we going to do?"
I said, "I don't know. I'm not sure what to do."
Cindy said, "I know, lets put it on YouTube! This is so weird."
I said, "Lets not. We don't know what's happening and it's not that interesting to watch. We should just wait and see if anything else happens, and then we'll go from there."
She said, "OK, but this is super freaky. Let's watch it again!"

She was excited, I was curious, and also at the same time a little worried. What in the world would cause the camera to move on its own? My "got-to-fix-it" curiosity was starting to kick in, but I wasn't sure if this was going to be something that I could figure out.

CHAPTER 10

Real Magic

I got home early from work and immediately collapsed on the couch. It had been an exhausting day and I needed a short nap. I was so tired I fell asleep on the living room sofa even before I finished my after-work-beer. After a while, I woke up and felt better but just a little light-headed. I had the same disconnected feeling I'd felt when I wake from one of my "falling" nightmares. I sat up from my nap and in front of me, on the coffee table, were a few magic tricks that I had left out from practicing the night before. I thought it was a mess and time and decided to clean it up. As as I began reaching for a dice cup, and before I could touch it, the cup tipped and started rolling towards the end of the table. My immediate thought was, "That cup is going to fall if I don't catch it." It then rolled off the coffee table and then, ever so slowly, it fell to the floor.

The slow-motion fall didn't immediately affect me as I was still in a half-awake state. It seemed slightly curious and was more a strange feeling and less about what was happening. "Wow," I said to myself. That was weird." It seemed to fall so slowly. Then, as I reached for the cup on the floor I thought, "I've got to pick up that cup."

Amazingly, as I reached, it rose off the floor and into my hand. "What! Did that just happen?" I sat there looking at the cup. Then I thought to myself, "This is crazy, I need to try this again." I placed the cup back on the table and held my hand over it. In my mind, I thought about picking it up. I concentrated, and slowly the cup lifted to my hand. Oh My! Did that just happen?"

With this discovery, I sat there on the couch for nearly half an hour. I tried it over and over again. It occasionally worked and sometimes it didn't. I then tried raising some of the other magician's items. A dice, a playing card, and a hollow metal sphere. I found out that smaller items were not that difficult, but the large items felt impossible to rise. This new thing... it was fun, and also exhausting. I could float or move something to my hand only if I imagined myself holding it. It seemed to work like static electricity. However, whatever item it was, it also felt like a great weight, a weight as heavy as a medicine ball stuck on the end of a stick. And, I couldn't hold anything up for too long. However, the more I practiced, the more I thought I was getting better at it.

I had some difficulties too. As I experimented, if I lost concentration, or if I was distracted or anything at all, I'd lose focus and it wouldn't work. Any moment of diverted thought and nothing would happen. The hardest part I found was, concentrating without thinking. You never realize how many thoughts go through your head at any given moment. Not exactly how many thoughts, but how thoughts bounce from thing to thing to thing. Like a ping-pong ball in a tornado.

There's the current idea in you're head. Then the noise outside, then, the thing on the floor, the cell phone, what's for dinner, last night's movie, the itch. It never stops! It's as though the whole world conspires to rob us of our attention. I knew that, if there was a technique to keep this concentration focused, I'd have to find it, and isolate it. That is if I could even manage to do it again. In no time at all, I had exhausted myself and fell asleep again on the couch.

I woke later in the afternoon and frantically texted Cindy at work. "You've got to come over tonight!" She texted back that she had made plans to meet some girlfriends after work for a quick drink. I insisted, "You've got to come over. It's important. I want you to see something." She said, "See what?" I didn't tell her what I had done. I just insisted I wanted to show her something. She finally agreed to come over after she met with her friends for a while.

I could barely contain my enthusiasm while I waited for her to arrive. I paced the floor and sent her a couple of reminder texts. I tried to watch TV but just kept flipping through the channels. She finally showed after what seemed like forever. It probably wasn't that late but the waiting drew the time out into eternity.

She walked in smiling profusely and a bit wobbly. It was the obvious effect of a martini or Cosmo or two. I sat her down on the couch and she watched me intently. She began to have a look like the fear of a girl who would like to get married but doesn't want the proposal to happen on a couch. I said, "I can't wait to show you this."

She fearfully raised an eyebrow and said, "What are you going to do?" I set a hollow metal magicians ball on the coffee table.

She then complained rather loudly, "Oh My Gawd, you didn't get me to rush over here just to watch you do some stupid magic trick!"
I said, "No, no... Just watch."

I sat down next to her and stared at the metal magicians ball, brought my hand close to the top of it (they're hollow and very light), and thought about making it move. Cindy watched. Then she started wrapping her hair around her finger like I'd seen her do a million times before. She was probably thinking about sex. Seeing her do that, I started thinking about sex. Then, I tried concentrating harder. Nothing. Nothing was happening.

I then said to her, "You may not believe this, but, I was making

the ball move, even float this afternoon."
She said, "Geez, you mean a magic trick? Like your bottle cap trick?" She seemed somewhat relieved it wasn't a proposal, yet annoyed it was just a magic trick.
I said excitedly "Yeah, exactly like the bottle cap trick. But without any props."
She said, "What do you mean? Like, for real floating? Really?."
I said, "Yeah, for real."
Her, "Bullshit. I don't believe it. Ok, so why can't you do it now?"
Me, "I don't know. I mean I really want you to see this. But, something's different. I don't have the same feeling I had earlier. I'm not sure what's different."

I sat back on the couch. I was excited yet still feeling fatigued from the day and frustrated it wasn't working.

Cindy said, "I'm going to get a beer from the fridge."
I said, "I'll take one too."

I took the cold beer from Cindy and went over in my mind the discoveries that had happened earlier in the day. I took a swig of the beer and leaned my head back. Cindy sat in the chair next to me and started to twirl her hair again. I thought about the afternoon. Right now, I'm feeling a bit disappointed and tired. Good thing was, the beer was starting to help me relax. Then, as I sat, I realized it. Earlier in the day, I was very relaxed. Now, I'm far too excited. When Cindy got home I was so very anxious to show her. I wasn't allowing my body or mind to feel the weight, the lightness, its mass, the heaviness, the connection between me and the ball. Right now, my brain was racing. There were the distractions of Cindy, the details of the day, and other random thoughts. All these were clouding my head.

Realizing this, I put my beer down, sat up on the sofa, and closed my eyes. I tried to relax, calm my brain, and relax my body. I concentrated on removing all thoughts out of my mind. I ignored the fact that Cindy was sitting near me, twisting her hair and slowly sipping her beer. I ignored the thoughts of me moving things around in the afternoon. I thought only about the ball and its size, and it's weight. I reached forward and concentrated on it. Concentrated on my hands, my arms, and the space between me and the ball.

Suddenly Cindy stood and gasped. Her beer dropped to the floor. The ball had risen about 4" off the table. Then, with a lite tap it hit, then rolled and fell off the table. Cindy had broken my concentration.

Cindy, "Oh my Gosh! You did it! You did that? How did you do that? How did you make that ball go up?"

I was rubbing my arms and felt a physical wave of tiredness came over my body and I felt a bit groggy.

"Damn! Matt, what the heck? I can't believe what I saw! What is this? How? Is this some super magicians trick you've thought up?" She asked. "It's really good."

While still recovering from my mental exertion, I said, "No, it's not a trick. I'm not sure how this is happening. It's still a bit of a mystery to me. I only figured it out this afternoon. And I've been practicing all afternoon. This is new to me, that's for sure, and I'm not sure how it works." She said, "Well I'm very impressed. But you say you don't know how it works? "No," I told her.
Cindy said, "Well maybe it has something to do with this house. I've always felt that this place was a little creepy." I said, "I'm not sure. I don't think it's anything with the house, but I don't know. Also, I think I don't want anyone else knowing about this, just yet. At least till we figure out what it's all about. Maybe it IS something that has to do with this house. Anyway, I also want to see if I will be able to do it again. Maybe I'll try again tomorrow or next week. I don't know if it will even last. But, I'm so glad you got to see it. But, right now, I'm feeling a little tired and I've got to get some sleep tonight."

She twisted her hair slowly and said with a little pout, "But it's not even 11:00." I took her hint, smiled at her, and said, "I'm going to bed, let's go." I grasped her hand and lead her into the bedroom. She followed me in and even as tired as I was, we let her martini's and cosmo's work their magic.

The next morning, as we got dressed for work, we talked about the previous evening.

Cindy asked, "What do you think made the ball float?
I said, "I have no idea, and I wish I knew. Remember I told you I've always had dreams of stuff floating, even my body floating for as long as I can remember?" She said, "Yeah, you've told me a few times. You say they are mostly in your nightmares. I wonder if your bad dreams and your problems sleeping have anything to do with it. But, maybe it has something to do with this old house? What do you think?" She continued, "You know what? At work, we have a sleep lab. There's a doctor there I could talk to. I could ask him about sleeping and dreams and nightmares."

I said, "OK, but please don't tell him anything about the bedroom video or the floating or anything. Just mention the sleep interruptions and nightmares. Do you promise?? She promised, "I won't, but I will talk with him. I know you don't sleep well, so maybe, if anything, he might be able to help."

Over the next several days, Cindy's schedule had been moved to night shifts and she wasn't able to come over for my much looked forward to evening rendezvous.

During the following nights of her absence, nothing out-of-the-ordinary or out-of-place occurred. Even the bedside camera hadn't turned on. Nothing odd, nothing unusual. The return to single life made me feel a bit lonely and I was missing her company. Those were long nights for me. The only way I could effectively fall asleep was to drink my regular shot of liquor, or even two, just before bed. I had grown accustomed to her being

THE FLIGHT OF THE MAGICIAN

next to me during the night. Then, a few days later Cindy came over before she went to work.

Cindy said, "Matt, "I was able to stop by the sleep clinic and met a "Dr. Johnson." He seemed like a nice enough guy and I explained to him that I had a friend that had some problems sleeping. I asked about dreams and floating dreams and sleep in general. He told me tons of stuff but said to truly evaluate some-one, he'd need to talk to you in person. He happens to have an opening tomorrow, in the afternoon. I said I'd see if you could stop by. He also said the first consultation is free!"

Me, "Well the price is good, why not?" She said, "Good, and guess what? I don't have to work tomorrow. So... I can stay here to-night." That, for me, was very good news to hear.

CHAPTER 11

The Sleep Clinic

The next day I met Cindy at the hospital just before her shift started. She introduced me to the sleep doctor, Dr. Johnson. Dr. Johnson was not quite what I expected. With the name Johnson, I expected a middle-aged white guy in a lab coat, maybe sporting a thick set of reading glasses. Dr. Johnson, however, was of Indian descent. He wore a turban and spoke with a thick accent. He did, however, sport a perfectly pressed lab coat. He was a nice enough guy, very pleasant with a measured, meticulous way of speaking which, I thought, would probably help anyone fall asleep. Maybe it was a trait of the trade.

He was, despite his steady way of speaking a rather jovial and warm professional. As we talked with him, we eventually would come to guess that he had probably heard every sleep-related joke that has ever been spoken out loud. And then, he would proceed to repeat them at every opportunity.

For example, he'd say, "I've always been so sleepy, whoever speaks at my funeral will probably just look over at my casket and say, "Well, he was always kind of looked like this." Also, "I'm so tired, when I get out of bed in the morning my favorite place to go, is back into another bed." And, "What did Sleeping Beauty say to Prince charming? Just 5 more minutes."

We checked in at the main desk and walked to his office at the hospital.

Dr. Johnson greeted us, "Hello again Cindy. Hi, Matt? Is it? Have a seat."

He insisted we call him Dr. J which gave me a mental image of an Indian Hindi rapper. I chuckled to myself.

Me: "Yes, It's Matt. Hello, nice to meet you."
Dr. J: Nice to meet you too. So Cindy tells me you have problems sleeping?
Me: Yes, actually it's been a problem for a long time.
Dr. J: Well, what can you tell me?
Me: Since I was young I've had restless nights and frequently wake up in the middle of the night. Often, I'm very hot and sweating.
Dr. J: That's not too unusual. What do you think is causing the restlessness?
Me: I don't know. Over the years I've had lots of upsetting dreams. Sometimes they are worse than others.
Dr. J started asking a barrage of questions: Do you drink caffeine? Work out before bedtime? Eat well? Any physical problems, pains, past illnesses? Do you have any work or added life stresses? Any addictions?
Me: No, nothing in particular. I'm pretty normal. However, many times I think I wake up hearing noises at night. And, many nights, when I wake up, I feel odd. (At that moment I thought about breaking my own rule to Cindy about not talking about floating things. Anyway, I did.) Sometimes I feel like I'm float-ing." Cindy started staring at me with a curious look on her face. I knew what she was thinking. "I sometimes up wake startled and feel like I've been flying or something. That's also when I often wake up, usually in a sweat.
Dr. J: "I see. Well, floating or flying, is a very common dream sensation. Sometimes, it can denote a feeling of happiness or of overcoming a burden. If you're scared or afraid while dreaming, you may have a fear of lack of control with something in your life. Are you able to control your dreams?"
Me: "Control my dreams? Well, I don't know. I've never tried to

control my dreams." For some reason, I didn't want to tell him at that moment that I've tried to direct or control my dreams for a long time. Especially after I've awoken to a nightmare.

Dr. J: "Why don't you give it a try? Next time, when you realize you're dreaming, try to mentally control what happens. It's called "lucid" dreaming. Many people practice it. You'll be surprised what you can do while sleeping. Many have solved problems at work, invented things, and some can dream their way out of a nightmare and change it to a happy ending. You'd be amazed."

Cindy and I turned and looked at each other. I thought to myself, "Wow, I thought that was something that only I had ever done, and there's even a name for it. Who knew that it's was such a common thing?"

Dr. J continued, "I also suggest, that for the next week, you write down a log of your sleep patterns. Write down the times when you go to sleep, when you wake up, and why you woke, if possible. As well as anything else you can remember, like, your feelings, sweating, muscle fatigue, cramps, pains, room temperature, what the dream was about, and so on. Also, make sure your bed and pillow are comfortable. You should also try taking a warm shower or bath before bed and I'd suggest no caffeinated products from noon on, and minimal alcohol. Keep the room temperature cool, but not cold. Most people sleep better when warmed by the covers while breathing in cool air. It helps with body temperature regulation. Come back next week and we'll see how you're doing."

Me: OK, Dr. J. That seems like a good plan.

As we drove home Cindy asked, "'I thought you weren't going to mention floating?" I said, "Yes, I know. But I didn't mention "I" floated, did I? I just told him about my dreams. I want to see if we can figure out these late-night disturbances on our own and why I sleep so badly before we try to figure out this floating stuff. If I'm able to get to sleep better without pounding a few beers or shots of liquor before bed, I'd love it." Cindy then asked, "You do what before bed?" I then said, "Well sometimes I have a drink or two, to help me get to sleep. But anyway, the floating may have just been a fluke occurrence or something to do with the house, so let's wait and see if it continues."

The following week I did as Dr. J asked and kept a log of everything about my sleep habits. I laid off the caffeine but kept my nightly beer or shot routine. I even tried to reduce the amount of alcohol, however, it had always helped me get to and stay asleep through the night. Without it, falling asleep could be difficult.

CHAPTER 12

Mike Needs a Girl

It had been a couple of months since Cindy and I had started dating, and Mike was still the third wheel. He was not an overly annoying third wheel lately, however, I mostly felt sorry for him. Cindy and I were always together and I thought we would have more fun if we were two couples hanging out instead of a two plus one.

I had tried to get him to read my attraction book but he hadn't. So, I thought that, if I can make Mike a little more interesting to girls, then maybe he'd be able to hook up with someone and we'd have more "couples" dates. I approached Mike with the idea that if maybe he could learn a magic trick or two, the girls might be more interested in him. He agreed and said that he would give it a try. We arranged to meet at a magic shop the next day to pick out an easy trick for him to learn. Mike was a little wary, maybe a lot more apprehensive, about trying to learn any sleight of hand so he decided he would buy one trick from the store, and then I'd teach him another simple bar gag. That should be enough to start him off.

In the magic shop, we went to we looked at one trick after another. As we rummaged through the store, Mike spotted several pairs of glasses on a display table. One pair was a Groucho Marx set with wide-brimmed black frames and an attached mustache. Another set was "X-ray" vision glasses, which turned out to be nothing but an optical trick where they made you see double. There was a pair of magicians "card reading" glasses which allowed you to see a normally invisible, luminous mark on the back of a pre-marked deck of cards. And, they looked just like ordinary sunglasses.

Mike picked up a pair of glasses, gave them to me to wear, and said, "Hey, look at me. Can you see through my clothes?" It was a pair of x-ray glasses. "Nope," I said, "But I do see two of you." He then found the poker cheater glasses and handed them to me. "Perfect." I thought. An easy trick for Mike and it takes minimal skill. Now he can read every card in the deck. No matter what card is picked or how bad his sleight of hand is, he's going to get it right!"

With the new "trick" glasses in hand and a specially marked deck of cards, we headed out of the store.

Mike: "Hey Matt, want to get something to eat?
Me: "Yep, lets head over to Keegans. We can practice your cards and glasses."

We sat down in a booth and Mike pulled out his new deck and glasses and started reading cards and acting like a magician. After a few minutes of reading cards, I thought it was a good time to teach him a simple bar trick to add to his magic repertoire. I decided he should learn the leaning salt shaker trick, as it was an easy one.

Me: Mike, I think you will need another trick to perform, and I know you've seen me do this one before, but you might not have ever noticed how I do it.
Mike: OK, that's a good idea. What is it?
Me: It's the leaning salt shaker, here's how it works. First, ask your victim to balance this salt shaker on only its corner. Here, you try.

As hard as he tried, Mike couldn't stop the shaker from toppling over. "All right, now let me try." I showed Mike the following steps.

I "accidentally" sprinkle a tiny bit of salt on the table, then discretely push it with the palm of my hand into a mini salt pile. Then, I carefully lower the shaker on that mini salt pile, balancing, until I'm just able to let it go. I gently raise my hands and the shaker is standing on edge, on its own.

Mike watched me then continued to watch the shaker standing upright on the table. Eventually, Mike says, "Oh, now I get it." Meanwhile, at that same moment, as I finished the trick, I noticed that I was feeling rather relaxed. I think while doing the trick I had to mentally calm myself and steady my hand while trying to balance the shaker. Just then, I got a whim. Still feeling relaxed, I closed my eyes and put one hand over the shaker and began to concentrate. I felt it's weight, the heaviness of the salt, the glass, and the curve of its metal top. With eyes closed, I mentally visualized
the shaker and without actually touching it, I willed it to float up. The shaker rose a short distance from the table.

Mike was astonished. He said, "Man! That's incredible. Awesome! I've seen you do that trick with the bottle cap. But, wow, you need to open your eyes and look at this!"

At once, the shaker fell to the table. Mike handed me the card reading glasses that he was wearing. Then he said, "Here. Check this out. Look at the shaker." As I put on his trick glasses he commented, "There was this purple haze around the shaker with the glasses on. It wasn't there until that shaker rose off the table."
With the glasses on, I looked at the salt shaker. Then Mike asked me, "Do you see it? It's got a purplish swirl around it."

As I looked, I saw a faint glow, like a transparent swirling vapor going around the shaker. And as I watched, the fog looked to be rescinding closer and closer to the shaker. Then, in a moment, it was gone. Nothing was left to see but the shaker, and a little bit of salt on the table.

"Wow," I said out loud. "What in the hell was that?"

Mike said, "That's a fantastic trick. Why does it look so cool through my glasses?"

I said to Mike, "Mike, I have no idea."

I proceeded to tell him about my "floating" experiments that I had discovered at home.

"Mike, for a little while now I've been practicing floating magicians balls and other objects. And, now this shaker you just saw. And by-the-way, it's not a magicians trick."

He said, "I don't get it."

I told him, "If I'm in the right frame of mind, relaxed, calm, and not too tired, I can make stuff move." Mike just stared at me. "And, I've been practicing. I learned I could move very light-weight things at home, like my hollow magician's balls. Just now I did the same thing. I did it to this shaker. I can float some other things too, but, I can't do it for too long as it gets tiring fast. I also think I'm been getting better at it."

Mike responded," OK, so these tricks you do are real? Like some kind of crazy mind control?"

I said, "Yeah, I guess that's what it is."

Mike, "Wow. Can you do the shaker again?"

I said, "OK. I think I can. I'll give it a try."

I put my hand over the shaker, relaxed, and closed my eyes. I started to get the feeling again. I sensed the shape of the shaker, the weight of it. Then I heard Mike say, "There it goes."

Still wearing Mike's glasses, I opened my eyes to a squint to see the shaker a few inches above the table. I also saw a transparent purple fog, so light it was barely visible, surrounding the shaker. I let the shaker down easy. The fog remained for a few seconds then disappeared.

Mike said, "That's so fricking incredible."

I felt a wave of exhaustion pass through my body, and after several seconds, my energy started to return.

Mike said," With those glasses on. Did you see it? It's got a purp-lish swirl around it, right?"

"Yep." I said, "I saw it. What in the hell is that?"

Mike said, "I don't know. But that is a fantastic trick. I wonder why it looks so cool through my glasses?"

I said, "I wish I knew."

He said, "I don't get it. Now, what are you going to do? Start a real magic show?"

Me: "Well, for right now, I'm not going to do anything, or tell anyone, and neither are you, OK?

Mike agreed, "Ok. Whatever you say. Hey, are we going to the club this weekend? I can try out my new tricks. How about an-other round?"

CHAPTER 13

Sleep Disorders

It had been over a week since I had started writing down my sleep habits. I recorded my sleep times, how well I slept, what I had for dinner, etc. Most nights were usually uneventful except for a random wake to noise or to something that had fallen over in the house. However, one night I woke from an unusually terrifying nightmare. I was jarred awake with what felt like a bash to the head. There was also the feeling of what could have been a small tremor in the house. My head was pounding and I was hot and sweating. I looked around the room and saw the red light on the bedside camera. It was recording. I went to check the video.

I backed it up to where it had started recording. As I watched, I saw myself lying on the bed. I could see that the sheets were quivering. After a few moments of watching, I saw myself rise several inches over the bed. I was shocked! Then, it looked like I woke up with a startle and fell to the mattress. The rest of the video was me sitting on the side of the bed, then walking over to the camera. I watched the video several times before pulling out the media card. On the way to the kitchen,

I grabbed a towel out of the bathroom and wiped down my sweaty body. I then poured myself a scotch. After quickly downing the scotch, I went back to bed thinking that Cindy had been right. She had seen me floating over the bed that one night. I wonder what caused me to float? I thought back to the salt shaker. Maybe something like the shaker is working on me when

I sleep? Maybe there is something in this old house that's affecting me? The camera doesn't lie, does it? And then I wondered if I should tell Cindy. Or, would telling her cause some kind of problem between us? The thought that she might get scared and not want to spend the night here anymore entered my mind. That was something I didn't want to happen. As I laid back in bed and thought, the scotch did its intended job. I quickly went back to sleep.

When Cindy came over the following evening I showed her the video.

Cindy said, "Oh my God, Matt. That's exactly what I saw awhile back. Do you remember? I don't think you believed me at the time."
I said, "Yeah I remember that time. Last night I was having a very intense nightmare, but I don't remember what it was about." I've been keeping some logs as Dr. J. suggested. I've got to find out why I'm having these experiences. Can you get me in to see him again soon?" I asked Cindy to make us an appointment to go see Dr. Johnson and she said she'd try.

Fortunately, w were able to meet with Dr. J. the next day.

"Hello Dr. J. I've brought my sleep logs with me." I gave him my notes.

He greeted us and after a short review of my notes. He said, "Good to see you again Matt. It looks like you've been very meticulous in keeping your logs. I bet you'd make a great doctor. Did you know that once I had been offered a job at a mattress factory? I told them I'd sleep on it! Hahaha! After his chuckling eased, he asked, " So, how's it been going?
"Great, I been sleeping fairly well."

Dr. J. "That's good to hear. Did you know you can use your Ipad to help you get to sleep? Yes, you can. There's a "Nap" for that! lol! Hahaha, OK So you've slept pretty well?"

Me: "I've cut back on the caffeine, especially in the afternoon and evenings. And I've been taking a hot shower just before bed."
Dr. J, "And work is good? And, you and Cindy too? All good?"
"Yes, everything is pretty good."

I was just about to start to elaborate on my odd experiences and frequent nightmares when then there was a knock on the door of the consultation room.
"Come in" Dr. J announced.

A very attractive staff nurse entered. She was tall and thin with straight blond hair and was sporting what I thought was overly red lipstick for someone working in a hospital. As she entered she looked directly at me and gave me a big smile. She handed Dr. J some paperwork to look over and sign. She was very pretty. I couldn't help but look at her a little bit too long and I think Cindy must have noticed me looking. I could feel the heat from her gaze even though she was sitting behind me.

Dr. J, "Oh, let me introduce you to Liz. Liz, this is Matt and Cindy.

As Liz took the paperwork from Dr. J, she continued looking at me and smiling. And then, only for a second, seemed to notice Cindy.

Dr. J. said, "Matt here is trying to sleep better. Can you imagine that?" And then he laughed out loud.
Liz laughed too then looked at me and said, "Well, we wouldn't want Matt to miss any sleep at all now, would we?"

We guys chuckled at her hidden sexual innuendo. Cindy folded her arms.

Liz, "Best of luck getting a better night's sleep, Matt"
Dr. J, "Thank you, Liz."
Liz said, "Nice you meet you all, Goodbye!"
Cindy broke her silence and snarkily said, "Goodbyeeeee."
Dr. J. "Now, Where were we? Oh, Yes, you're sleeping better now? Yes?

I then decided to let him in on my nighttime wake-ups.

Me: "Dr. J. I do still take a shot of liquor or a beer before bed. I normally can't fall asleep without it.
Dr. J: "OK, not good, but I understand. What else?"

Me: "Well, I often wake up with a start. And, it's usually in terror."
Dr. J "Oh really? Explain"
Me: "Sometimes I have the sensation that I'm floating, or, I have the sensation of flying. Not like flying in a plane or a vehicle, but only me, just my body. And I usually end up begin startled wake when, in the dream, I can't stay up anymore. I start to fall and can't stop falling and can't control the fall. That's when I wake up. I feel afraid, and also, I'm always sweating."
Dr. J: "So, falling dreams. Is this the same dream every night?"
Me, "No, I remember a few. In one dream, I'm flying through the air in a Jetliner and then see an obstruction ahead of lots of thick suspension lines. Like guy wires from a super tall radio tower. I dream I'm working so hard, trying to fly, and trying to miss all those wires. I know I need to fly between them and if I can't, something bad will happen. I'll dream of trying not to hit those wires or I know I'll come crashing down. Another dream is, I'm either floating or flying over a housetop. Rolling through the air and rolling around trees, like I'm body surfing at the beach. It feels like catching a wave and riding it into shore. Up and down, at first, like a smooth roller coaster. It will be pleasant to me, that is, right up to the point where I'll start falling, knowing I'm going to hit the ground and be hurt or worse."

Dr. J, "Hum, interesting. Do you remember I explained to you that many people have the sensation of flying while sleeping? It's very common. There are many possible associations regarding flying or levitating in dreams. Besides expressing anxiety, It is also not uncommon that it can be a very positive experience. It can be an expression of great freedom or happiness. You seem to have the more negative of the two. In your case, it could mean you're trying to overcome a feeling of unworthiness or a personal problem. Then again it may also be a sign of control. Do you say you're having problems staying afloat in your dreams? Do you have any personal issues you're trying to deal with right now? Family? Work? Money? Cindy?"

Me: "No, aside from my not sleeping well, everything is really good right now. Work is great. Money isn't a problem although I always want to have more. My family is doing well as far as I know. They're mostly out-of-state but they would let me know if anything was up."

Dr. J, "Cindy too, I take it? Is she stressing you out? Ha-ha! We both glanced at Cindy. She looked back at us rather disapprovingly.

Me, "Yep, she's great. So far." I say with a smile.

"I'm the best thing that's ever happened to you!" Cindy replied.

Dr. J laughed at her comment.

I hesitated for a minute and said, "There is one odd issue that I'm experiencing."

Cindy looked over to me and mouthed silently, "Matt, no."

I looked over at Cindy and said, "Well, I need to tell somebody sometime."

Cindy leaned her head to one side and said, "All right."

Me, "Dr. J., I had told you that I had dreams that would often wake me up, dreams of flying.

Dr. J. "Yes, you've mentioned that."

Me, Well, for as long as I can remember, even as a child, I've had these flying dreams. Lots of times, I've been frightened awake by nightmares. Nightmares of flying, or falling. And, so far, I've just put up with them. I'd just shake it off and go back to sleep. But lately, it's been getting a lot worse. And, this worries me a bit, but, the other night, I think I was actually... floating."

Dr. J, "Really... What do you mean, floating? You dreamt you were floating?"

Me: "No, not a dream, but, actually floating. It was real. We even have a video of it happening.

Dr. J, "Really??!!" Dr. J leaned back and stared at me, eyes wide.

Me, "Yeah, that, and some other stuff too. I can move things. Move them without touching them."

Cindy chimed in," Yep, he's right, I've him do it, more than once!"

Me, "Just small things, and, only on occasion."

Dr. J turned to Cindy, "Cindy, is your boyfriend having some fun? Dr. J stepped out of his doctor's serious mode for the moment and we could tell he wanted to start laughing.

Cindy, "No, let him show you."

Dr. J. remarked, "OK, I'd love to see. I've never heard of anything like this."

Me, "I'll try, but I'll let you know, it doesn't always work. Do you have a quarter Dr. J? I'll use one of yours so you'll know it's not some trick. And I won't touch it at all so there's no swap out or, or anything."

Dr. J, "Sounds good but I don't have a quarter, but here, how about a dime? You guys are really raising my curiosity."

Me, "A dime is even better. The lighter it is, the easier. Just set it on the table. Right in the middle."

Dr. J, "This should be interesting."

I leaned back, I took a minute to relax, closed my eyes, then reached out and put my hands over the coin without touching it. Then, after a minute of relaxing and breathing slow, I started to get "the feeling." I could feel the dime on the table. I willed it to move upwards.

After a few seconds, Dr. J whispered, "That is amazing."

I squinted open my eyes. I saw that I'd made the dime float about 10 inches over the table. And it's spinning like a top. I ended my concentration and it rattled to the table.

Dr. J., "That has got to be the most interesting thing I've ever seen. Are you able to do it repeatedly?"

I say, "Yes. Sometimes."

Cindy expressively says, "I've seen him do it lots of times." I thought Cindy was being a little over supportive.

Me, "It does get tiring after a little bit. And, there is this video we took. It shows me floating. I'm floating over my bed. At least until I wake up."

Dr. J. leaned back and started wringing his hands and then commented, "Floating over a bed? That, I'd have to see! Oh my! This is a very interesting development. I'm not sure how to proceed. This is something I've never dealt with before. I'm not sure how or why this has anything to do with your poor sleep, but, this is certainly unprecedented. This is hard to understand. I'd greatly like to see that video."

At that moment, I had the intrepid thought that if I showed him the video he wouldn't believe it. He might take it as some computer-generated video trickery.

Dr. J., "If what you're saying is true, then we'll have to do some research into what's going on. I'm sure that we'll need several, possibly many tests. Is it all right if we can get you in here on a regular schedule over the next few weeks? With you're permission and cooperation, I'd love to understand what is happening. We need to discover what mechanisms are at work. I must tell you I'm very excited. I think I may not sleep well myself over the next several days!
Do you happen to know a good sleep specialist?" Ha-ha!"

Me, "Well, I'm good with trying to find out what's happening, however, I think don't want anyone else to know what we're doing. I mean, I don't know if we should tell anyone about this because it's all too weird. I want to see if we can figure this out first. This ability may be temporary and may go away. And, it's all a little bit overwhelming."

Dr. J. said, "Not to worry Matt. I understand your concern and we'll keep this between ourselves. I do keep a good lock on patient-doctor confidentiality. And, I'm as curious as you are. I can't wait to start the research and look forward to meeting with you soon."

As we finished our consultation with Dr. J. he explained that he needed to do some study before proceeding with my case. Cindy agreed to bring him the video of the floating incident. We made plans to meet in a week and then said our goodbyes.

CHAPTER 14

Feeling "The Feeling"

It wasn't even a couple of days later when I got a call from Dr. J. He asked me to come in as soon as I could. Both Cindy and I were free the next day so we told him we'd come over tomorrow. He was happy to hear that and set the appointment.

The next day, after we signed in we, entered his office and you could tell he was extremely excited. He had us sit down and started telling us what he'd found.

Dr. J.: "Good, good to see you. Here, have a seat. I've been researching and studying and been so busy I can hardly contain myself! The video Cindy brought me, if it's not a hoax or some kind of trick, then it's truly incredible. Just incredible! My initial thoughts were, to see if I could find if anything like this ever being recorded. What I've found is, there's been at least 130 years worth of real experimentation and scientific research on these types of abilities. There is such a thing relating to this and it's called psychokinesis or telekinesis. However, even though all those years of testing and research, there has never been a reliable, repeatable demonstration reported. The only thing that has come close proving telekinesis has been a variety of magician tricks and man-made special effects. But, they are only illusions and tricks.

I was, however, amazed at the eagerness that people have had to find out any evidence of these kinds of abilities. There have even been a couple of offers of big prize money for anyone who can demonstrate any proof of psychokinesis or telekinesis. For example, James Randi, a professional magician, has offered a one million dollar prize for any person who can demonstrate any kind of paranormal event, like levitation, telekinesis, or mind-reading, in a controlled mutually agreed upon experiment. And so far, no one has been able to claim the prize.

Incidentally, with regards to that, I must tell you, Randi did do something funny one time. At one of Randi's shows, a person trying to claim the $1M prize had actually beat the tests! What he did was, using a computer and some electric arm sensors on audience members, tried to guess a chosen card from a deck of cards. He did it! He then blindly drew a picture that was randomly selected from a gallery of photos, once again, selected on a computer by audience members. He did it! Then, he drew another picture of a geometric shape that was hidden in a sealed envelope. On that test, he made James wear a helmet with sensors, and Randi chose an image of his selection, then sealed it in an envelope. The claimant got James' picture right. He passed all the tests! And, to Randi's agreement!

Then, at Randi's insistence of delivering an immediate check for $10,000, with the remaining $1M prize to follow, both the claimant and Randi congratulated the audience. Then they said, "It's truly amazing that someone passed the tests. And on a day like today. What day is it you ask? April 1st. It's APRIL FOOLS!" HAHA! And the audience erupted in laughter. I Love it! Do you get it?? April Fools!"

Dr. J. laughed profusely, "It was all a big joke! Do you get it? Well, OK I thought it was very funny." Dr. J laughed some more, then explained calmly. "But it is, however, a bonafide challenge offered by Randi."

Cindy and I weren't as amused by Dr. J.'s story as he was, but it was clear that he had certainly done some research.

Dr. J. went on to explain, "Seriously, another time, an Eng-

lish businessman, Gerald Fleming, back in the 1970s, offered 250,000 pounds Sterling to the then famous Uri Gellar to see if he could bend a spoon under controlled conditions. Uri, at the time, was famous for being
able to bend spoons just by using just his mind. Yuri refused to accept the challenge even though bending spoons was what had made him famous.

Then, there was the magician Houdini, who loved to bust so-called "psychics" as scammers. Even after Houdini died, his wife tried to contact him for years with seances and psychics, but to no success.

I also read that there was supposedly a lot of research done by the Soviet Union in the sixties and seventies regarding psychic experiments. There were claims of successes using telekinesis and remote viewing of distant locations, but, then again there is no substantiation to any of those claims or experiments. However, there have been a few good movies made from those rumors. And, I do believe the research was indeed done.

So... from what I've found so far, there is nothing to help me explain your... your condition.

That being said, as for now, what I'd like to do is to start with a full physical, some basic scans, blood work, etc. I want to get some stats on you. I'll start with blood work and I'd like to get an MRI scan done right away. I'd also like to keep a video log of your talent, but right now, I'd like to see you do one of your levitating tricks again. Do you think you can do it?"

Me: I think so. We went into another room where Dr. J had already had a video recorder set up. There was a table in the room with a couple of chairs on each side. He started the camera. I did the floating "dime" trick again, in the same manner as I did before, but this time I used a quarter.

Dr. J.: "Fascinating, simply fascinating!"

Cindy had to leave to go to work after the coin trick, so she said her "goodbye's" and left. Dr. J and I then started with the health screenings.

Dr. J ran a series of normal health checks, a heart stress test, reflex tests, and with great reluctance I even let him draw a little blood. If there is one thing I can't stand, it's needles. I hate them. Everything so far went smoothly, that is until we checked into the MRI scanning room. It was in there that I began to doubt my choice to go along with all this testing.

He asked me to undress, then wear the always fashionable hospital medical smock and then instructed me to lay on a tilting MRI table. I dutifully obeyed and as the table tilted back I was told to relax and to try and lie as still as possible. The technician also reassured repeatedly that, "This won't hurt a bit." This seemed easy enough to do as I was getting more used to relaxing on demand. I mean, every time I wanted to do one of my "magic" tricks, I had to relax and calm myself, to get "the feeling."

I willed myself to be very still and quiet. However, right when my head was starting to enter the scanner I heard a loud "tick." I felt a surge of electric power slam into me, through me, and my head felt like it was about to explode! Another "tick" and I pushed myself out of the machine screaming, not by choice but as a reflex. It felt as though there was a demon being forced into my body. I immediately fell off the MRI table. I had to escape what was happening and I had to do it fast! The technician and Dr. J both simultaneously yelled "STOP" and the tech ran over to me as the machine was shut down. I began crawling across the scanner room floor. My head hurt as though a car had been dropped on it. My vision was grey and I could only see things in shades of grey. The grey is what followed after the brilliant white flash and white floating orbs of molten light that shot through my brain at the moment of that first "tick."

Dr. J. came in to comfort me and asked. "Oh my! Are you all

right?"

I was dizzy and shaking. Shaking as though my nerves were having problems connected to my brain. The pressure in my head felt enormous! Blood ran from my nose. In those few minutes on the floor, I felt like there could have been no better solution than death. The technician tended to my nose and I was placed on a gurney. They must have given me a tranquilizer as I don't remember anything else until I woke the next day.

Dr. J and Cindy were both standing bedside when I woke.

Dr. J, "Hi there, you OK?"

I had a severe headache, but I could now see in color.

Me: "Yeah, I can see and hear you. Although I'm having a difficultly focusing. My body doesn't seem to want to move, my head is pounding. And my elbow and knee, they really hurt."
Dr. J. "Well, that's from you falling off the scanner table."
Me: "Ok, that makes sense."
Dr. J, "I don't think you reacted well to the MRI."
I stared at Dr. J. and said, "You think?"

Dr. J. "I've never seen anyone react, like you did, to an MRI scan. And a physical reaction to an MRI? Well, that just never happens. There should be none whatsoever. There have been nervous patients, fidgety patients and patients who had pain from their aliment during an MRI, but a physical reaction, that's unheard of. You created quite a stir for the scanner staff. They will be talking about you for a long time. I've had to refuse to let anyone from the other offices look or talk with you, although they've been fairly insistent. I absolutely must ask you again, although you answered "No" in all the initial paperwork, do you have any metal in your head? Or anywhere else for that matter?
Me, "No doc, no metal."
Dr. J. "Ok, Now, we can absolutely find out if you do, but, I have another test in mind."

Me, "Oh, wow, I don't know if I'm ready for that. Or, want to do any more testing. I'm pretty sure if it kept going, I was going to die in there."

Dr. J. "All right, then let us just do some observations, and, when you feel better we can try some other things. But for now, we'll wait until we are ready. I think it's really important that we find out what's going on in your head. It is, after all, the source of your thoughts and dreams."

Me, "We'll see. But, I don't want those other doctors or any-one asking me questions right now. And no more blood tests or shots! I hate shots. When I was a kid, my mother and nurses would have to hold me down. They had to hold me, kicking and screaming while trying to vaccinate me. I was so frightened that I'd twist and squirm and scream and they'd have to jab me 3 or 4 times to innoculate me. I'd kick and cry and the nee-dle would rip out. Once it even broke off! So, no more shots or blood samples. Your drawing blood was enough for me. I don't like shots and needles and that's that. And no more MRI's. I can't do that again, ever! Let's keep things simple, Ok?"

Dr. J. agreed, "All right Matt. We'll take it easy on the testing and sampling. I want to talk with Cindy for a minute. I want to give her some instructions on how to look after you before we re-lease you." I agreed, and he took Cindy out of the room to talk with her. After a few minutes, she came back in, asked me how I was doing and I told her, "I don't feel bad, aside from a persistent roaring headache." She told me to take a little nap and she'd look into getting me out of here. Cindy then left and I dozed off.

When I woke up, Cindy was sitting next to me doing something on her phone. She noticed I was awake and commented, "How are you doing sleepyhead?" I told her, "About the same. Maybe a little hungry." She produced a protein bar out of her purse. I finished the protein bar and after I had been up for a while, and everything seemed to be "ok." She made arrangements at the front desk to check me out of the hospital.

Cindy asked me as we left, "So you had a bad time in the MRI room?"

Me, "Yeah, they said it wouldn't hurt, but wow, it was the worst."

Cindy said, "That's really weird. I told Dr. J. I'd keep an eye on you. That's why they let you out so early. The hospital said they wanted you to stay in again overnight."

Me, "I'm glad you did. I don't like to be confined to a hospital room. The weird smell alone is enough to make me want to escape."

We laughed a bit and then Cindy took me home. After a dinner of hot-soup and under Cindy's watchful attention, we called it a day. I was glad to be at home, and I was glad she was there.

CHAPTER 15

Research

Several days later I was scheduled for another meeting with Dr. J
Dr. J., " Hello Matt. Are we feeling better?"
Me, "Yes, however, I did have a rather persistent headache for a
couple of days. Now, I'm fine."
Dr. J, "Good, good. Please tell me if anything changes. Let me tell
you what I've been doing. I've been doing lots of research, and
the results are rather interesting, although, I still haven't found
a comparable example for your case yet.

What I've discovered is, Telekinesis and flying are curiously
common subjects. Throughout time, there have been numerous reports of people that can fly or levitate. One of them, for
example, was Prince Hussein who was reported to fly around
while sitting on a magic carpet. King Solomon was supposedly
able to fly from city to city. I found a Russian folk tale where
Ivan the Fool would sit on a carpet and be able to jump across a
river.

Now, one of the more plausible accounts is of Buddha, who was
claimed to be able to walk on water or levitate over a stream
with his legs crossed. Several other yogis have also been reported to be able to levitate. There was an Indian Yogi who on
June 6, 1936, was said to have levitated for several minutes in
front of a large crowd. With all these reports, it's a really common phenomenon.

Even if you look back on Christianity, Jesus was said to have walked on water to meet his disciples, who were in a boat. And if you continue along the Christianity timeline, there have been any number of saints over the years that were said to have been able to fly, or levitate, or walk on water. In fact, there are so many reports of people levitating, that it's hard not to think that some of them, at least a small percentage, might have accomplished it. The stories are so common, it makes one think it must have

been done. The biggest problem, however, is evidence of proof.

Speaking of proof, I've got a camera here in my office. Do you mind if I try filming you doing your coin trick once again?"
Me, "Sure, I'll try."

Dr. J. readied his equipment and when he was ready he motioned for me to "do my thing." I focused on the coin. The coin stood on up on edge, then fell over.

Me, "Ouch, ouch, ow! I can't do it." My head started to hurt. "Sorry, Dr. J. It seems that, since the MRI, I haven't been able to do any of my lifting tricks. When I try, it starts an instant headache. It just hurts my head too much right now. I've tried a couple of times, and what I just did was better than what I could do yesterday. But, I think it's coming back, slowly."
Dr. J. "That's OK, Matt. That's interesting, and good to hear that you're headaches are lessening. I would hate to think that we caused any permanent damage. I am very interested to find out what's going on. I believe we have a landmark case with you. What we need to get is more substantive data. Is there any chance I can get you to try an X-ray?
Me, "Oh no, I'm not sure that's a good idea."
Dr. J. "Well, I'll tell you. X-ray machines use an entirely different method of photography to see into you. It's not at all like an MRI. See, the "M" in MRI stands for "magnetic," Magnetic Resonance Imaging. MRI's work by spinning up the molecules in your body with a very strong magnetic field then using very sensitive sensors to detect the magnetic decay time of the molecules in

the different organs. All very technical I know, but the bottom line is, it works magnetically. I would have loved for the MRI to work as we probably would have gotten much more information. But, it must have been those magnetic pulses that caused you your severe and unusual reactions. X-Ray's work differently. X-rays are extremely short bursts of radiation. And with those pictures, we may get at least some look of what's going on inside you. What do you say? Are you as curious as I am?"

Of course, I was curious! Knowing that I love to know how things work is irresistible to me. Yet, I still had some apprehension. Me, "OK, let's give it a go. You're right, I am also super curious. But I can't do anything like that MRI again. No way."

Dr. J. took me to the X-ray lab. Once again, I've put on another fabulous peep-a-boo, butt crack revealing medical robe. He had me lay down on a table and put a heavy lead-lined towel over my "family" parts. Over the table was a long white arm that loomed over me with a large white box on the end. And the white box had one big black eye staring at me.

Dr. J walked to an adjacent room and said, "I'm going to do this myself and I want you to lay as still as possible, OK?"
Me, "OK, just let me know before you start."
Dr. J "Yep, already took the first one. Everything OK?"
Me, "Oh? Oh yeah? Sure. I'm fine."

The big black eye rotated methodically down the whole of my body and spent a particularly long time circling my head. I felt that at any moment it was going to do something random and smash into me or my head. It didn't. The procedure was nearly silent and the rest of the session went well. It was nothing like the MRI!

Dr. J. "There we are, all done. Still, feeling fine?
Me, "Yep, I feel OK"
Dr. J "Great, I'll have these worked up quickly. I can't wait to see the results. Let's meet again in a few days. I'll have time to go

over these and do more studies. And, hopefully, you'll be feeling even better."

CHAPTER 16

Stranger Things

Along my recent visits with Dr. J., life was moving along pretty much as usual. I had work during the day and Cindy was working odd shifts at the hospital. The weekends were usually hanging out with Cindy, and Mike, often going to dinner, then out to a club, or at our favorite sports bar. Every once and a while we would catch a baseball game or see a movie. It had been many days since I had headaches and every so often I'd "practice" my magic tricks. I was getting better and the hollow "magicians balls" had gotten so easy that they required almost no effort at all. Coins were easy too. I could even float a tennis ball or baseball, however, I found that my hands needed to be much closer to them to make it work. I was even able to make one of my dining room chairs dance.

One evening while eating at home alone, I sat at the table and practiced pushing the dining room chair next to me back and forth. I'd set my hand out toward the chair, then relaxed to get the feeling, and, with my hand only a few inches away, was able to move the chair. I pulled it back. Pushed it forward, pull back, push, pull, push, then I tipped it forward and then backward on two legs. Lastly, I made it stand up on one leg and spin. After doing all that chair dancing, I was feeling rather proud of what I could do. And after a good dinner, and the following wave of exhaustion from doing those tricks, I slept very well that night.

On Friday evening I was invited to a house party at one of my client's homes, Chuck and Kathy. They were one of my best clients and happened to be a very nice couple somewhat close to my age. They were married and both worked and owned their accounting firm together. They told me there would be a good crowd that evening and it should be a lot of fun. I think they may have thought I was single as I've never worn a wedding ring and I had never talked to them about any personal matters. Because Cindy was working the second shift that evening, I asked Mike if he'd like to come. I had done a good amount of work, expensive work, at their house during that day as well as earlier during the week. They wanted their home to look great for the party, inside and out. New bushes, decorative stones, a Japanese style rock garden, fresh mulch. etc. I also wanted to show off my work to Mike, maybe get some praise from the homeowner couple, and, if lucky, maybe even get some referrals. I figured it would be a good opportunity for Mike to mingle, me to network, and there would be food and drinks. "Why not give it a try?" I told Mike. And, if it gets boring and we want to leave, their place wasn't too far from our usual hangouts.

Mike and I arrived a little late and, as Chuck and Kathy had said, there was a pretty good mix of people there. Mike was particularly happy as there was indeed a good amount of un-escorted women. I think we figured that Kathy had invited all her single friends. I thought, isn't that just like what women like to do? If a gal has a single girlfriend, then everybody tries to fix them up. Anyway, Mike and I mingled around and there were lots of introductions and unfortunately not so much interest in the landscaping as I had hoped.

After about an hour, three gals walked in and one could tell that they were dressed to impress. To watch them as they came in together, however, was rather comical. All three looked so much alike, you'd think they'd been interviewed as the backup band for a Robert Palmer music video. Similar clothes, similar makeup, similar shoes, similar... everything. They were all wearing tight short miniskirts, all black, but not the same. Black pumps, varied. Two of them were wearing white shirts and the other, a wide striped black and white shirt. Two had highly highlighted blond hair and the third, long dark black hair.

All three of them were wearing similar blingy jewelry, and all had bright red Lipstick. I could imagine the "pre-going-out" conference call they must have had while they were getting ready, "What are you going to wear? I don't know, what are you going to wear? I'm thinking of wearing this, or maybe that? You? Maybe that instead..." And what eventually happens is that the girls, most of the time, end up dressing so much alike that they resembled three, walking, talking mannequins in a store window, showing off variations of the same designer. I wondered if they had any idea of the effect they made, dressing and looking so much alike. Amusing! I had to laugh.

There were three bodies, one mind. Then, immediately, I recognized the tallest blond. It was Liz from Dr. J's office. At the moment I saw her, she saw me, and came rushing right over with girlfriends in tow, "Matt! There he is!" She gave a big unexpected hug, kissed me on the cheek, and then introduced me to the other mannequins. I could tell by her slurred speech and the slight scent of alcohol on her breath that they must have started their evening earlier at some happy hour somewhere. Liz stared intently at the other two girls for a few seconds. They both grinned at each other, pursed their lips, then excused themselves to go find some drinks.

Liz, "Hey there, how have you been? You know Charles and Kathy!?"
Me, "Hi. I've been great. Yeah, Charles and Kathy are clients of mine. I completed a large project for them today. So, you know them too?"
Liz, "Oh great. Yeah, Kathy has been one of my best friends from... way back when. You know, school days. So far back that

I don't want to tell you how long. Hahaha! It's so good to see you here!" She was almost singing. "I was hoping I'd see you more often at the office. How's Dr. J. been treating you? Are you feeling better? Is your girlfriend here?"

There was a barrage of questions coming from her, at me, all at once. I could tell she liked me, but I also thought the alcohol might have been a factor. Me, "Dr. J is great. He's very attentive. Although you got to know, his jokes aren't all that funny. I've had several appointments lately and also have several more scheduled soon. And, Cindy, couldn't come out tonight. She's working."

Liz responded, "Oh, too bad for her. And yeah, Dr. J's jokes, I think I've heard them all... several times each I think." She rolled her eyes and moaned at her statement. "I can't wait to see you at the office again. Are you getting everything taken care of? When is your next appointment?"

Me, "I'll be there Wednesday, and I'm fine and doing better." I didn't want to tell her what we were doing at the office. "Dr. J and I, well, we're working on a special project. Some testing, and some studies. I'm sure I'll run into you there at some point. At one of my appointments."

In the back of my mind, I was thinking I'd better shake this girl off before some word of me talking with a tall blond made its way back to Cindy. It was bad enough Liz was there and being rather forward. Cindy would not approve.

I thought I'd shove her in Mike's direction. A little buddy to buddy assistance. I said, "Hey Liz, let me introduce you to my friend Mike. And, why don't you introduce your friends to him? He IS single."

Liz perked up, "Is he rich? Or really good looking?" I could sense that her girl radar was put on high alert. If there is an available man in the room, then a single gal definitely wants to know more about him.

Me, "I'll let you and your friends decide. He's over here."

I led her to Mike and introduced them. From then on, I spent much of the evening trying to avoid Liz. Although every time I looked around the room, I felt like she was watching me. Twice, she came over and tried to refill my drink. I declined and quickly made an exit to the bathroom or outside to hopefully talk about my landscaping to whoever was there.

As the evening progressed I was beginning to feel the effects of a long hard workday. I was feeling a little tired. Mike was talking with a gal that, I'm pretty sure, worked as a dental hygienist. I had overheard her say, "I never drink anything that can stain your teeth. Like coffee, tea, or dark sodas. That's why I mostly drink vodka." Ha-ha! That made me chuckle. Earlier, Mike had used the magician's card reading glasses to perform a card trick for a group of girls. It had worked. He was actively engaged with this girl and she seemed to be laughing and having fun. Which was a good thing!

Over my dating years, I've noticed that gals seem to laugh too much when they like a guy. Guys do it too. I had read in my dating books that girls will show interest when they like a guy. They'll be giggly and laugh at just about whatever the guy says. I got very curious one day, and read up on why people laugh. I mean, what's the point? Does it serve a purpose? Besides expressing fun or surprise, why laugh? One of the theories in psychology is, that humor evolved to indicate interest in existing or potential relationships. What I found in this scenario was, it's universal that laughing is a commonplace observation in human interaction. That is, with friends, family members, allies, romantic partners, or strangers, etc., people use humor to initially judge or test social standing as well as to test interest. If someone is interested in forming a relationship or to be accepted, then they're more likely to act interested, that is, smile and laugh. If they don't laugh, then they probably don't want as much interaction. He was talking, she was laughing. She was talking, he was laughing. There was relationship interest testing going on. It looked like they were hitting it off.

While Mike was "interacting" with the hygienist gal, I was starting to feel a bit drained. I decided I might be able to relax for a few minutes on the sofa. I settled onto the couch with my beer and every once in a while I would glance over at Mike. He'd give me a nod and a smile. They seemed to be hitting it off well as she was
still talking to him. "Wow, good for him," I thought. "Maybe this one will stick around."

The party was going strong and many people were milling around. This had turned out to be a popular party. I needed to take a break for a few minutes as the day had been long and exhausting. I was hoping to take a step back from the crowd and disappear for a few minutes and relax. From my seat on the couch, I could see, on the opposite sofa, an average looking, pale, balding, "accountant" type guy wearing a white dress shirt and black jacket and jeans who was talking with a slim, very attractive black girl. She had medium short curly hair and was wearing a short, tight sexy gray dress. She was very cute. Too cute for him I thought, not that it mattered.

As I sat there on the sofa feeling relaxed and comfortable, I started to get a little sleepy. In the din of conversations and background music, I was starting to tune out a little bit. I saw that Mike had left his Magician's glasses on the coffee table so I decided to put them on. Maybe with the glasses on, as they were fairly dark, I wouldn't appear bored or tired. I took a big swig of beer and leaned back to relax.

I woke with a start. I was having the same kind of fearful, panicked feeling that I get when I have my falling nightmares. I realized I had unintentionally drifted off to sleep and I felt a little embarrassed to have jerked myself awake. I looked around to see who might have seen me. I saw no raised eyebrows, nobody laughing... Cool. Nobody saw me. I glanced at the couple that was still on the couch deep in conversation across from me. The accountant was leaning far forward intently listening to the pretty girl's story.

I thought to myself, "Man, he needs to sit back and give her some room. He's invading her personal space and I can tell that it comes across as he's too interested. It's creepy and needy. The pretty girl was excitedly explaining about some accident where she was nearly crushed or fell or got hurt. She then said rather loudly, "Oh no! I feel like it's happening right now. I'm so light-headed!" My attention switched from the accountant to her.

She reached up and put her hands on each side of her head as she was talking and reliving her story. I noticed a smokey, semi-transparent, purple cloud of fog hovering close to her head. It kind of looked like a mini purple galaxy. As I watched that fog, I could see images. Fading in and out was a fairly clear vision of what she was talking about. It was like a video of the event she was describing. The event was out of focus sometimes but I could see a bookcase full of books, like in a library, that fell over and narrowly missed hitting her.

I then realized I was still wearing Mikes glasses. I took off the glasses, no purple cloud. Glasses on, the foggy disk and a fallen bookcase image, but now the fog was fading away. Odd. What the hell is this vision thing? And, holy cow! What? Now I can see thoughts? Maybe because I was so groggy I was just thinking about her story and projecting it to myself. Like in a dream. I looked again with the glasses on. The fog had faded away. At just about that time, Liz came over and plopped herself down so close to me that I got a face full of blond hair and almost spilled my beer.

I got up off the sofa. "Hey there! Where are you going? Are you being a party pooper?" Liz chimed. "Yeah, I've got an early morning tomorrow." I was lying. "You have a good evening," I said to her. Liz pouted back to me, "Aww, you don't have to go yet do you??" "Yes, I've got to go. Have a good time." Liz frowned her disappointment, "OK, but I hope to see you at the office soon." I got up and found Mike and said to him, "You can stay, but I'm going home."

CHAPTER 17

Stranger Nights

The following Saturday, Cindy, Mike, and I had decided to head out together for the evening. Fortunately for Mike, the girl he met at Chuck and Kathy's party, Phyllis, had given him her phone number, and said she'd meet him out. Yay! Finally, a double date.

Cindy and I went to Mike's house first, then out to one of our regular dance clubs. Mike's date was already there waiting for us. As soon as we saw her I think the three of us were thinking, "Awesome! So good so far... she showed up!" It was a busy night and there was a pretty long line of people at the door already. Mike, introduced Phyllis to Cindy and me. And, since we had become regulars there, we went straight to the front of the line and introduced her to Jim, the doorman, who knew us well. Jim allowed us to go right on through. This was good for Mike as he was immediately scoring some big points with Phyllis right off because we got past that long line of people. Then, as soon as we walked up to the bar, the bartender had our favorite drinks ready and waiting for us. The bartender then asked us what our ladies were drinking.

There's nothing like a little VIP service in a popular place to impress a gal. A few of the other regulars we knew stopped by, or waved and said Hi. Mike's girl was impressed and Cindy was happy to have another girl to talk with. We knew it was going to be a fun night.

We all downed a few drinks, danced a few dances, and had fun and good conversation. Cindy and I entertained ourselves with the promising romance of Mike and Phyllis. As it started to get late, the club became even more crowded. Cindy and I decided this would be a good time for us to exit. Mike and Phyllis were so involved that they had nothing but tunnel vision for each other. So, with Mike doing well on his own, Cindy and I decided to leave and get some alone time. We said our goodbyes, during which I whispered to Mike, "Tomorrow, I want the full detailed story about tonight. Don't fuck it up, go for it, and don't be a pussy. OK?" With that encouragement and a punch in the arm to Mike, Cindy and I left.

When Cindy and I got home, we made a trail of clothes from the front door, across the living room, and into the bedroom. We spent the next few hours kissing, caressing, and doing the "horizontal dance." Front to front, front to side, sitting bedside, standing behind her bedside, my hands on her shoulders having my way with her as she absorbed my maleness. What a great night! We laid together, curled up close, with her head on my shoulder, exhausted, satisfied, and relaxed, and we fell asleep.

I must have started dreaming. At first, I saw myself performing a standing chair trick in front of an audience. I had called them all together just to impress them, show them what I could do, and that's the only reason they were there. In my dream, it was my exposure to the world of what I could do. I felt so confident, even braggadocios. I concentrated hard. Then, in my dream, the chair, it wouldn't move. The people watched and I could see them start to fidget. My trick wasn't working. Damn! I was so upset with myself, confused, frustrated. The crowd of people was starting to get annoyed with me. They were scoffing. Since the chair trick wasn't working, I decided to try one of my metal magicians' balls. That, I knew I could do. But now with the ball, again, the trick wasn't working. It was the same result, nothing moved. The ball just sat there. Why was this not working?

I could feel the anger and disapproval of the spectators. This show was wasting their time. Why was I was a failure? I felt despair and frustration. "Didn't they know what I was trying to show them?" Then, my dream changed.

This dream was one I have had before. Now I was a pilot of a jetliner full of people. It was in mid-air, cruising through open skies. Everything seemed to be normal. Then, there it was, off in the distance. I could see radio tower support wires. Long, thick gray wires leading from an enormous, ridiculously, impossibly high, red and white radio tower. A tower that was so tall that it couldn't possibly be a real structure. Yet, there it was. And those wires. Thick, yarn spun metal. Giant strings of gray floss in the sky, durable enough to slice off a wing, tear off a rudder, or cut through the fuselage. And what's this? Now I could see, in the distance just within sight that the wires were both diagonal as well as horizontal to the ground. It was an odd tangle of metal ropes, but there were openings, gaps in that grey spider weave. We were approaching and approaching fast. As I was piloting I thought, "I'm going way to fast to turn around, and we're far to close to go over. It's impossible to go under or around. It looks like I'm going to have to fly through. I'm going to have to some-how get this plane between those wires or this plane is going to be chopped up. And if I fail, there will be streaking flotsam of metal chunks flying through the air, some on fire, arcing to the ground. People will scream and fall to their death. Those wires meant fear, failure, devastation, and sadness if I couldn't find a way through them.

I felt desperate. Got to do something now! Urgent! I had only seconds to decide. Is there space enough, yes? I think I see. But, it's not big enough. There, there's another, and over there, an-other. But which one should I choose? The lower gap? No good, we'd end up crashing into the ground. The upper gap? That's got to be it, there's no alternative. I pull back on the stick and feel the plane angle up into the air. The weight of my body pushes into the seat. I struggle with the controls. The yoke is heavy in my hands, and it's fighting back. The jet angles higher. "Damn, you heavy ass pig. Move! Come on, get up to that gap. Engines at full throttle. "GO, go, go... come on!" I try to will the plane up and I feel a great weight and anxiety as I realize, "We aren't going to make it! Watch out! I wake up to the sound of a loud thump!

Matt!

Cindy screamed. I sat up sweating, looked around, and saw Cindy sitting on the floor. She's was crying. "What the hell did you do?" She asked.
She was looking at me and rubbing her elbow, then her head.
I asked, "What's wrong? What happened?" I got out of bed and came over to look at her injuries.
"I fell to the floor." She sobbed.
I said, "Oh no! What happened? You're sitting in the middle of the room?" I was asking but at the same time struggling to wake myself up and make sense out of what just happened.
"You dropped me!" She whined.
"What do you mean I dropped you?" I said,
"Well, you were carrying me to the bathroom, and then you threw me down." She said angrily.
I told her, "Oh baby, there's no way I did that. I was asleep. You just saw me get out of the bed." I was trying to figure out what she meant. "There is no way that I could have dropped you."
"Well, I woke up when I hit the floor. And now my elbow hurts, my knee hurts, and my head is sore."
I brushed the hair out of her face and tried to see her injuries.

Then it hit me, "The camera! Cindy, the camera light is on. Let's take a look and see what it recorded if it recorded anything."
"OK, but I need an aspirin or something. And if there is a bruise or scar I'm going to be so pissed. You're a jackass. I'm just letting you know."

I played back the video. It had indeed recorded something. 30

sec, 1 min, 1 min 30 sec, almost 2 minutes worth. I watched the little screen while Cindy went into the bathroom, got some aspirin, and a drink of water. The camera view started out pointing at the bed, and on the far side of the bed, there was the dresser. I could see the two of us lying there as she laid back down, everything black and white in the night vision of the camera. Then, the video clicked off, then on again. I saw Cindy slowly rise out of the bed in the same position she was sleeping in. The bed cover slid off of her and her big hair was draped down around her head. Still sleeping, she fidgeted a bit as she rose upwards. She floated past the camera as her body continued to slowly get higher. She floated towards the middle of the room and exited the view screen. After a few more seconds, just before I got up to tend to her, there was a loud thump.

I rewound and played it back to her. "Oh wow! Did you see that? You lifted right off the bed. Nothing was touching you. And, can you see me still sleeping?" I commented to her.

We both watched it again. We could see that I was asleep but probably dreaming. The look on my face was tense like I was worried. We watched her rise from the bed, totally unassisted.

Cindy said, "That's creepy! I was sleeping, but dreaming you were carrying me! How did this happen? And why in the hell am I floating around? This is just way too weird. And these bumps, they hurt like shit. And I'm going to have bruises. Dammit, I'm going to have bruises!"

I said to Cindy, "This is so strange. I WAS having a nightmare, I remember it. It was about me performing tricks and then flying a plane. I was feeling so stressful, and look at me, I'm so sweaty. This has to be something to do with my floating tricks and my nightmares. Maybe the way I've been able to move things around lately, my tricks, it must have worked on you while I was sleeping. But, I wasn't thinking about you at all."

Cindy, "Well you better not do it again. It fucking hurts."

"Hey! I'm telling you, this wasn't my idea. I'm sorry, but I don't know how this happened. Maybe it is this old house, or I have something going on that's way out of my control. I'd like to know what's going on."

Cindy: "OK, but I'm going to go sleep on the couch. And, you're staying in here."

Despite her demand, we both fell asleep on the couch.

CHAPTER 18

Pineal Evolution

After that night's episode, I changed my appointment to see Dr. J. earlier than we had scheduled. He was eager to see me and had already planned to call me to have me come in at my earliest opportunity. I arrived at his office at the hospital and signed in. Before I could find a seat in the waiting room, he came to the front desk and greeted me. He then immediately whisked me straight to an examination room.

Dr. J: Hello, hello Matt. Please come in, we've got so much to discuss with you. I'm so excited. I've discovered some really interesting developments. First, I've seen the x-rays and have had some time to review them. They are fantastic! I mean it's fascinating. Let me show you."

He was so excited. He was jetting around the examination room like coffee was the only thing he'd had to drink for two days. He pulled up four of my x-ray headshots, and one from someone else. He also put up a cartoon-like drawing of a brain and started poking a pointer at them.

Dr. J: "Let me tell you about your brain. The majority of your brain looks fairly normal, however, there is something very, very interesting in your slides." He pointed to the other person's brain picture."OK, now this is a normal brain." I took a look. Then he said, "The vast majority of your brain is pretty insignificant, Ha! No, not insignificant like boring or unimportant, but insignificant as normal. For the most part, your brain is pretty much standard as far as brains go. However, it's this difference here that makes me very excited. See this area?" He pointed at the middle of the cartoon-like brain. "There is a "deep" structure here. A small gland in the center of the brain called the Pineal gland. See it? Everyone has this gland."

Me: "Ok, I see it." (I looked at where his pointer was touching.)
Dr. J: "Now, here is the same gland on your x-ray." He pointed at the middle of my X-RAY headshots. "If you were to remove this gland and take a close look, it resembles a tiny little pine cone, about the size of a peanut. Thus the name Pineal (pine-E-AL.) And, strangely enough, as small as it is, it requires an unusually large amount of blood supply for such a tiny organ."
Me: "Oh yeah, I think I see it." (Although, I really couldn't really tell what he was talking about.)
Dr. J: "Ok, Now look at your pineal. It's quite a bit larger than normal, see that? It's very large. Actually, it's extremely large! And, there's more.

But first, let me explain to you about the brain in general and the Pineal.

The brain is an organ that begins to develop in the womb, then through childhood and even continues to develop into adulthood. The consensus is that the brain doesn't fully finish developing until your late 20's, even to the late 30's. Which is exactly where you're at. The brain has many parts, such as the hemispheres, frontal and pre-frontal cortex's, lobes, the brain stem, and many other parts. All of these parts perform many functions, whether it's sight or hearing or motor skills. That is, most parts are known to be assigned different duties, that is, except for the Pineal.

This gland is somewhat a mystery, and it is known to produce Melatonin. Melatonin has an important role in maintaining our circadian rhythms. It helps us regulate sleep patterns, that is, our sleep and wake cycles. The Pineal is said to also help regulate the pituitary gland and its secretion of sex hormones. But, there's no concrete evidence or research to confirm this. It is also thought to help regulate some other hormones as well but in reality, it's not fully understood. The Pineal is somewhat of an obscure, mysterious gland.

The Melatonin production aspect, however, has been confirmed and its production is directly influenced by light. Most commonly, daylight. Because of this reaction to light, it is often referred to as the "Third Eye." Now the Third Eye is thought, by different beliefs, to have many kinds of functions. The Third Eye is said to, "See what might be. Imagine the future. Or, see inner realms or spaces. It's also said it can be used to see energy, like aura's. There is even speculation that it functions as a doorway to all things psychic - telepathy, lucid dreaming, astral projection, and even telekinesis! This is interesting stuff, yes???"
Me: "Yes, pretty much." I could see the fascination in his eyes. He was absolutely intrigued by this stuff.

Dr. J, "There are also neural connections to the brain from the Pineal. Scientifically, it's not known why, but they are there. I believe they must be there for some reason. As I always say, there's a reason for everything. But for the Pineal, I can't say exactly what that reason is.

Now there's more... take a look at the area around your Pineal. Do you see it? Above, around and in front of your Pineal?" I said "Yes," But I still couldn't make out one thing from another. Dr. J, "In most brains there is a cavity area right there in the middle, surrounding your Pineal, with fluid in it. That fluid is called Cerebrospinal fluid. Most doctors think that this fluid is used mostly for shock protection, kind of an interior liquid-filled cushion for the brain. If your head is hit and your brain gets jarred, this fluid is there to help prevent or at least mitigate the damage."
Dr. J. hit the palm of his hand on his head several times. I thought he might actually hurt himself.

"For you, however, see this area? The ventricle around your Pineal? It's nearly full of tissue. It seems to be of similar density as the Pineal and appears to grow into and around it. This is incredible! And, at the same time a bit worrisome. In most cases, if I saw this growth, I'd say you have a neoplasm or some kind of tumor. But in your case, I can't say for sure. It could be a neoplasm, or a cyst, or some calcifications. Or, it could be some other structure that I'm not familiar with. It appears to be attached to the Pineal, but I can't, for sure, be certain.

What we should do is invite a specialist to help us out in assessing what is happening in your brain. Don't get me wrong, I am knowledgeable in brains, it comes with the territory. But, these structures are beyond what I can diagnose. In your case, we need a specialist. I know of
a neuro-specialist who's kind of a rock star in his field. Oh yes, did you know that the sleeping brain has a favorite rock group? It's called REM! Ha!" Dr. J started laughing as usual. I laughed too and rolled my eyes.

Dr. J continued, "Well, that's kind of funny. Where was I? Oh yes, a specialist, I'll contact him and check to see if he's available to meet with us. I'm sure he'd be interested in your case. I know it's the most interesting thing that I've ever seen, and it's not even my specialty. I'm sure he'll insist on helping us and can assist in trying to better understand your... your condition."
Me: "Ok Dr. J. I think its a good idea, but I hesitate to anyone else know about this. I understand it's all very fascinating and I may be an interesting case study for you, but until we get a handle on what's happening, I don't need anyone else to know. I'm not looking forward to becoming a specimen or curiosity for doctors to poke and prod. And, I don't even know if this "affliction" will last. But now that we've talked, I'm concerned it may be physically bad for me. Is it going to make me sick or something? Like you said, is it a tumor? I'm certainly as curious as you are. I will tell you that I do like being able to do those lifting tricks.

However, there is something else I think I need to share with you."

Dr. J "Oh really? What do you have for me?"

Me: "Well, there are two things. First, I've found out, that if I use these magicians' glasses, (I showed him Mike's card reading glasses.) I can see a purple glow around the things I levitate."

I handed him the glasses and he viewed them carefully.

Dr. J. "Interesting."

Me: "And last night, in the middle of the night, Cindy fell in my bedroom. And, I think it was because of me."

Dr. J asked, "Hmm, Tell me why do you think it was because of you?"

Me: "Well, I'm not sure exactly sure how it happened, but what I know is, I was having a nightmare about flying when, in the middle of that dream, I woke up to her scream. That's when I saw that Cindy had fallen to the floor, because, um, because she had been floating in the bedroom."

Dr. J leaned far back with an amazed expression and asked, "She fell because she was floating? I'm not exactly sure what you mean. Is she Ok? How did this happen?"

Me: That's just it. I mean, I don't know. I was dreaming of flying, piloting a plane and when my dream ended, that's when Cindy hit the floor. I believe that, because I was dreaming about flying, somehow, that made her float off the bed. Just like she was one of my floating tricks. I have, right here, a video of her floating up, up off the bed.

I brought out a thumb drive copy of the video and gave it to Dr. J. He plugged it into the TV. We watched and viewed Cindy floating off and away from the bed.

Dr. J "That's incredible, simply incredible. I just don't know what to think. Is there anything else you can tell me?"

Me: "Yes, I think so. As of late, I can tell you that I have been sleeping much better, but now, all these new things are popping into my head. Here's what I'm talking about. I was at a party the other night and I fell asleep with those glasses on. When I woke up, I saw a girl across from me telling a story, and somehow, I saw what she was talking about. I mean, I imagined what she was saying. No, wait. Let me say this right. I think I could actually see what she was thinking."

Dr. J "Oh my! Yes! That sounds like the alleged mental capabilities of the Pineal. This is remarkable! I'm going to have to figure out how to test these things. I'll have to study some more, and figure out some kind of test series. I must tell you, I'm very excited! This is quite a development.

As, for right now, I've set up some equipment where I'd like to document some more of your lifting experiments. Is that Ok?"

I agreed, "Sure, if I can." We then went to another exam room and proceeded with testing.

For this session, I was able to perform with no problem. With electrodes attached all over my head, my arms, and chest, Dr. J started the recording equipment and over the next hour filmed me lifting different objects. He had even brought in a bowling ball (which brought him a slew of laughs.) Starting from light to heavy, I lifted - a playing card, a balloon, my magicians metal ball, an apple, a baseball, a basketball, a chair in the room, a table in the room, and lastly, the bowling ball. I wasn't sure if I could manage the bowling ball after all the other objects, but it wasn't too hard. Before Dr. J and I finished taping, there was a knock at the door and Liz entered. Her lips as bright and colorful as always.

Liz: "Matt! Hey there, I saw you on the sign-in sheet! Whoa! Is that a bowling ball?"

She broke my concentration and the ball struck the table.

Liz: "Was that a bowling ball trick? Can I see you do it? Did you teach Mike that card trick of his?"

Dr. J "Hello Liz. How can we help you?"

Liz: "Oh yes! Dr. J., You wanted me to let you know when your next appointment arrived. They are here in the waiting room."

Dr. J: "Thank you, Liz."

Liz: "Do you gentlemen need assistance? Anything at all?" She said while staring at me.

Dr. J, "No, we're fine right now."

Liz, "Ok. If you do need anything, just let me know. And Matt, stop by the desk and say hi on the way out?"

Me: "Ok, Liz, will do."

Liz left and Dr. J carefully labeled the videos in envelopes. He made notes and asked me questions about how I was feeling during the session, how tiring it was, what were my sensations, what I was thinking about. I started to feel like we were headed in the right direction. Hearing the information about tumors and diseases earlier wasn't something that had made me feel any better. But now I felt we were doing something constructive.

As I left his office, Liz was at the front desk and was virtually impossible to dodge.

Liz: "Matt! Me and some friends are going to Rock Taco bar and restaurant next Thursday after work and it'd be great if you stopped by. I'll even buy you a drink!"

Me: I said, only trying to be polite, "Thank you, Liz, I see if I can make it."

Liz:: "Ok, great! See you there!"

I drove home and was feeling rather tired from my office visit and the stress of the day. Cindy wasn't planning on coming over this evening as she said she'd been put on the late-night shift for the next couple of weeks. So for tonight, I was on my own. After dinner, I decided to put on Mike's magic glasses and try one more lifting trick before going to bed. I had come to think that when I practiced my floating ability, I seemed to sleep better afterward.

I noticed the tricks seemed to be getting easier and easier for me. I laid a baseball on the table, relaxed, pictured the ball, and imagined the space between the ball and me, and the weight of the ball and what I wanted the ball to do. I then opened my eyes. Through the glasses, I could see a swirl of purple-blue haze encircling the ball. I mentally tossed the ball back and forth through the air. When I tried to send it too far a distance from me, it would drop. So I kept it close enough to control easily. I set it back gently on the table and relaxed. The blue-purple fog faded away. I was feeling tired from the food and the fun, and sat back on the couch and drifted asleep. I immediately started dreaming about "lifting" items on stage in front of a large audience.

I woke up to the sound of glass breaking. I looked towards where the glass was and saw, broken on the floor, the heavy crystal vase that I had given to Cindy for flowers. There was a mess on the floor of water, glass, and flowers and as I looked at the broken pieces of crystal, with the glasses on, I could see a quickly fading, blue-purple fog.

I went to the kitchen and got the sweeper and bucket, to clean up. As I was cleaning the glass, I came to realize that, "It could be my thoughts that are the reason things in my house made noises or seemed to move on their own. It might have been me all along. After all this time, I'm the reason for the nighttime weirdness. It must have been me all along." As I headed to bed I made a mental note to myself, "Be careful of what you dream."

CHAPTER 19

The Third Eye

The next couple of days were routine. Work was going well and I was enjoying my regular schedule. I continued to practice my floating exercises in the evenings. And, I didn't have another appointment with Dr. J until the following week, however, he had informed me that a Dr. Shawn Ebb, a neuro specialist, was very interested in my case and would be joining us at my next appointment.

I decided to do my own search about the Pineal gland but wasn't able to find any more information than what Dr. J had found. What I did find, however, were some articles that suggested that Yoga and some other techniques can be used for relaxation and focusing inward. Some of these techniques were even said to exercise or strengthen the Pineal. One suggestion said specific-ally, "To enhance the Pineal, one should strive to have complete darkness when sleeping." The thought being, that if the Pineal gland is activated by darkness, then it will be deactivated by light. I also read that, it's possible, that the whole body can react to light. It turns out that light can stimulate all kinds of things in our bodies. I, however, was mainly interested in how it affects the brain and the Pineal. With this in mind, I made sure that my bedroom was as dark as possible when I went to bed. That my blinds and my bedroom door were closed and any source of extraneous light was blocked. Even my electric clock, Irma, was set to minimum display brightness, which meant "no display at all." And that was fine, as it worked by voice command anyway.

Some of the techniques I had found helped me calm the body, clear the mind, reduce stress, and supposedly awaken the soul. I developed a few of these methods into a good, short, relaxation routine that helped me to clear my head and relax. I was doing deep breathing, humming, and different yoga positions during my practice sessions. They did, with practice, help me to settle down my brain.

During some of my evening levitation sessions, I was starting to test the limits of what I could move and could not move. I'd start small, almost always with my hollow metal magicians' balls. But now, I was amazed that I could now lift more than one at the same time. After the balls, I'd try something heavier, like a chair, then the coffee table. After the coffee table, I placed one of the metal balls on it, relaxed again, then lifted the table with the ball in the center of it. I'd mentally tilt the table and try to make the ball move around, but not fall off. I was able to make it go back and forth, then around in circles. It reminded me of a wooden Labyrinth game I used to play with as a kid. It was so much fun, I spent a good amount of time doing it. I then got out my bowling ball. The idea of practicing on it, I thought, would be more exhausting than anything else I'd done. But that wasn't the case at all. It was more difficult than the lighter items, but only slightly so. I could lift it, and control it, and as long as I didn't think about the weight of it, I could keep it up in the air for quite a while.

After all the lifting and the resulting effort it took, I rested for a bit. But, I was so excited by the success of the bowling ball that I decided to get one of the 50 lb weights from my weight bench. I set it on the coffee table and thought, "This is going to be interesting, this thing is HEAVY! I'm not sure I'll be able to do it."

I relaxed and closed my eyes and started concentrating. I mentally visualized its size, and it's weight. Then, suddenly, with astounding speed, the 50 lb weight shot up in the air and slammed into the ceiling. I was startled and immediately lost my concentration. Smash! The barbell weight fell and crushed the end of the coffee table. My pet birds in their aviary took notice and squawked loudly at the sound of the crash. "Dang! I thought to myself." I sat back on the couch and looked at the damaged table and the barbell weight jammed through it. I had to think about it for a minute. "Why in the hell did that weight shoot up like that?" I replayed the sequence in my mind. I was expecting the weight to be heavy, really heavy. So heavy that I didn't think I'd be able to lift it. But, it had shot up in the air like a bullet. I thought, "Perhaps... perhaps it's because I expected the weight to be extra heavy. I must have overcompensated for it somehow." I picked up the weight and put it on the non-damaged part of the table. I was pissed my table was ruined.

I've got to try this again. But, this time, I'll go slow. I'll try to connect with the weight as it is, not as I imagine it to be. So I began to try again. I relaxed, closed my eyes, I started humming down deep in my chest as I breathed in deep and slow. I imagined the weight as though I was holding it with my hands, arms reaching out, even though my arms were relaxed by my sides. I closed my eyes and visualized the distance from the weight, to the table, to me, and felt the space in-between. I opened my eyes slowly to see that the 50lb disk had risen. I saw it, in the center of the room, rotating slowly.

It felt lighter than the bowling ball, even lighter than a baseball or a chair. I set it back down softly. "Wow!" I said out loud to myself. That was so easy. I wonder why? There's got to be a reason. My "got-to-know-how-it-works" mind was engaged. My metal magician's balls were very easy, but they were also hollow and super lite. This big heavy bench weight is also metal. Could that be it? Both metal? It is as simple as that? I decided to test this. I went to the kitchen, looking for something metal.

A knife? I laughed to myself. No, let's not experiment using knives. A spoon? Spoons aren't very heavy, so that's not a good enough test. A frying pan? This should work! Much heavier than a magician's ball and its metal. I took the frying pan into the living room. Once in the center of the room, I held it with an outstretched arm. I closed my eyes and relaxed and concentrated, then, I let it go. It was easy to float! Nearly as easy as a magician's ball. I opened my eyes to see it floating midair. It remained suspended there in the middle of the room. To me, it felt as though I could hold it there for hours. After a couple of minutes of watching it midair, I decided to grab it by the handle to take it back to the kitchen. At same the moment, I grabbed it, however, I had a thought, "I'll try to spin it with my thoughts, while I'm holding it." I wanted to see if I could mentally twist it out of my hand. Which would be stronger? My grip? Or my thought? So mentally, I twisted it. The pan handle broke my grip and spun around sharply and whacked my knuckles. Whap! Then the pan dropped to the floor. I started dancing around trying to shake the pain from my fingers. Ow! That hurt! But, it was a fascinating success. Wow, this is so interesting. It seems to be so much easier to lift things when they're made of metal. This is one more thing I can tell the doctors. It may be one more piece to the puzzle. But, damn, now I need a new coffee table.

CHAPTER 20

Decisions

For several weeks, I had practiced and tested my levitation tricks. I had also become better at coaching myself with Yoga and other meditation techniques to calm my mind and body. With all this practice, I'd convinced myself that this ability probably wasn't going away. The only thing I was curious about was how to make the thought visions work. I had done it once and was intrigued to see if I could do it again.

I had bought several pairs of those magic card reading glasses and had given Mike back his pair. I had them lying around the house like how old people do with reading glasses. I had a pair in the car, a pair on the "new" coffee table, pair in the kitchen, and the bedroom. I had them close so if the occasion arose where I might see a vision, they'd be available. I was now wearing them pretty frequently. And, they made for a pretty good pair of sunglasses.

I still wanted to keep my levitation a secret, but in the back of my mind, I knew I had to make a plan. It was either keep it a secret, tell only close friends, or maybe exploit it for profit. Another idea that I had was to submit this ability for research at a university or a medical lab. The curiosity of what I could do was picking at my brain like an itchy, unanswered question. But the thought of becoming a research subject was unappealing.

That is definitely what I didn't want to happen. Become a guinea pig, a lab rat in a cage. Who knows what kind of tests would be needed? And, probably lots more needles. Lots of needles! No way! I'll continue with Dr. J. After all, I've grown comfortable with him and I think we're making progress. I'll wait and see what he can come up with. In the back of my mind, I was still afraid it might be a tumor or some sort of disease.

As I thought about how I'd explain my abilities to others, I decided I might get some outside opinions or ideas, thinking this might help me figure out how to make some kind of plan. I decided to ask my friends what they thought about what I should do.

I met Cindy for lunch one afternoon and explained what I had in mind. She was silent for a minute then jumped up, "Let's have a dinner party! With Mike and Phyllis! It'll be fun! We'll see what they have to say about all this. And, we'll have a nice dinner too." I said, " That's not a bad idea. They already know a lot about what I can do. I'm pretty sure Mike has told Phyllis something as you know how couples tend to talk. Will you set it up?"
Cindy, "Sure. I'll do it soon. I've got something going, umm, that is, I'm busy at work for the next few evenings. I 'll have to check my schedule. I think I can plan it soon. Maybe Saturday night? Woohoo! A dinner party! It'll be great!"

That following Saturday we had Mike and Phyllis over for dinner and drinks. After a good meal and a few glasses of wine and after the usual banter about work, people, and the weather, I told them I would like their opinion about something.

Me: "Hey guys, let me show you a spoon trick."

As we sat at the table, they watched as I mentally lifted a spoon from the coffee cup in front of me. I spun it through the air, dropped it back into my coffee cup, and stirred it in a circle.

"Oh my God! " laughed Phyllis. "By Saint Bosco's cross. You do the best tricks!"
Mike clapped and laughed.

I said, "Well everybody. This is what I'd like to talk to you all about. First... Phyllis, I'm sure Mike has probably told you about what I'm been able to do? My ability?."

Mike looked down at his drink and Phyllis just stared at me.

I told them, "Let me start at the beginning. As I grew up, my younger years were not easy. My dad was a professional gambler and had supported us reasonably well when we were young. I mean, I was a kid and didn't know any better, but I had clothes to wear and never really wanted for much. But, he would be gone for long stretches at a time and I always hated that. He always seemed to do well when he was away gambling in the casinos. They used to say that he had a natural knack for reading people. I heard that the other players sometimes accused him of cheating because he won so often. That is, up until he died one night from drinking too much. At least that's what was said had happened. Then, after he died, to keep money coming in, my mom became a fortune teller, a medium, physic reader, whatever you want to call it.

I hated her for doing it. I always believed it was just an elaborate scam. I'm pretty sure she took people's money simply for listening to their problems and then telling them
what they wanted to hear. But, she had regular clientele that would stop by like clockwork. They'd swear that she could read their future and then they'd just hand over their money. At school, the other kids would call me Voodoo Matt or Magic Matt just because I was her son. Of course, I've gotten over that, but now it seems, the odd stuff has come for me.

For some while now, I've discovered that I've been able to move things. What I want you all to know is that - it's not a trick. When I concentrate on moving things, they do. This is not a magician's trick or illusion. This is, I'm sure, some kind of mind control. And right now, I'm trying to decide what I should do about it."

Mike said, " What do you want from us?"

Me, "I've thought about a couple of different scenarios that I want to discuss. Though I do want you all to know that I do have some doctors working on this. One of them we know through Cindy's office and he is bringing in another specialist. We've already started conducting some experiments and been recording my progress. He's also completed some basic medical tests and for right now, everything seems fine. But, there are some concerns that I've been grappling with and that's the reason I could use your input. So, here are my initial thoughts.

"One, we can try to make some money with this."

Mike piped up, "Wow! There's a great idea! Let's make a show with this! I can be your manager. We can travel the circuit, go to Vegas!"

Me, "Hold on there Mike. Let's think this thing all the way through. Maybe it's a possibility, and, I do want to get back to that.

Mike said, "OK, but damn, I think that's a damn good idea."

Me, "Next, I can do nothing and keep this ability to myself. I mean ourselves! Just keep on going to the doctors and have more tests and examinations. They might find an explanation for what I can do. And I think, ultimately at this point, that may be the best action. I'll explain why in a minute. But first, now, do you guys have any thoughts?

Mike asks. "Do you think you can teach me to do it too?"

Me, "Mike, I don't think it's teachable. I think it's something that I've been born or "afflicted" with. As I mentioned, it's not a trick. But for you, Mike, I will show you the magician's way of doing the floating cap trick. It's not that difficult."

Mike, "Well, I guess that will have to do."

Me, "OK, anyone else?"

They sat and thought for a minute.

Phyllis spoke up, "I think it's a little creepy. There is something not right, maybe even a little spooky about it. I think maybe you should stop it." She grimaced like she had just smelled something bad.

Cindy added, "It kind of freaks me out too. This is all so weird. I've seen a lot of it and, to tell you the truth, I'm a little afraid of, of, the weird things going on in here."

I looked her way, surprised.

Cindy started, "I mean, just the other night, we were sleeping..."

I cut her off before she could continue her story with a head shake and a disapproving glance. I knew she was about to tell them about the bedroom incident. I didn't want to divulge too much about what I could do, especially when I didn't know how to control it.

Cindy continued, altering her story, "And sometimes things move around here, in the house by themselves."

"And," I added, to further the diversion, "I've been practicing lifting things here, quite a bit."

Phyllis then commented with what seemed like a bit of contempt. "It's like, you're possessed or something. I mean, who does this? Nobody does stuff like this! It's supernatural or demon-like. I hope it's just you working on some magician's stuff or something. Otherwise, I'd say you need to be put in a monastery or jail.

Mike interrupted with a slight laugh to make a joke, and to derail Phyllis's worry, "Or put in a mental institution!"

We all laughed a little at Mike's suggestion. But, in my mind I was thinking, is this what might be going on? Maybe I'm possessed? That would be the weirdest thing. And, how would I know? The more I thought about it, the less that it seemed likely. It was my mind, when I concentrated, it was me that made stuff move. Not some otherworldly voice in my head that made me do it. It was an interesting comment though. She was certainly worried. Is this how the rest of the world would view it?

I told them, "I'm pretty sure I'm not possessed, Phyllis. But I think Cindy may be pulling strings around here from time to

time. As you can see, I have no control when I'm around her."
I was trying to make a joke to soothe Phyllis's worries. Cindy
then said, "Damn straight I am. You WILL do as I say!" Everyone
laughed at that.

So, any other thoughts?"
They all shook their heads, "No?" Nobody seemed to have anything more to add.
Me, "Ok, here are my options that I've come up with. For the
reason that I may want to ignore this is, for now, is this ability may only be temporary. In an extreme worst-case scenario,
it might even be terminal. Like a tumor or something. So, with
either scenario - terminal or temporary, that would be a good
reason to "not get used to doing it." I guess that would cover the
entertainment aspect as well.

Mike said, "Well, shit. No traveling show."
I told them, "I see no guarantee that we can count on something that could be temporary. And, Phyllis's reaction might be
normal for many people. They might be more freaked out than
entertained. So, I think the best course is probably to keep this
to ourselves right now. I'll maybe perform an occasional trick
or two to keep our friends amused. After all, most of our friends
are used to seeing me produce a trick every once in a while anyway. That being said, thanks for helping me get some ideas. For
now, let us keep this between ourselves. Ok? Great! Now, let's
get on with having some fun. Let's play some games."

We proceeded to play games and had a great rest of the evening.

CHAPTER 21

The Doctors

I met with Dr. J a few days later at his office. We began talking about his plans for tests when the new specialist walked in. Dr. J introduced himself as it was his first time meeting Dr. Ebb in person. Dr. J welcomed him, "Nice to meet you, Dr. Ebb. It was great talking with you on the phone. I'm glad you were able to take some time out of your busy schedule to meet with us. This is Matt." We greeted and then Dr. J began to recite to me a whole list of degrees and studies, associations, and papers that Dr. Ebb had earned that went way past anything I understood. Dr. Ebb seemed to be a nice enough man and certainly looked to be the typical doctor type. He was completely cut-and-polished like someone who might work at a high-end jewelry store. I could picture him selling diamonds to millionaires. And when he moved, he moved with a measured, conscious manner like a finely tuned watch. Almost robotic. He was athletically thin, late-fifties, and had brown/Grey hair with a haircut of someone that uses a military barbershop. His thin black-rimmed glasses made him appear even smarter than he probably was.

After introductions, Dr. J said he'd like to show Dr. Ebb some of my "talents" as that would be the best way to explain what my "affliction" was and where we were concerning our testing and studies.

We all walked to the exam room where Dr. J had preformed our previous tests. He called Liz on the intercom to bring something in for him. In the middle of the was the table that I had tilted at our last set of tests. Liz walked in holding a large box. Dr. J then asked Liz to put the items from the box onto the table. She pulled from the box, a large clear glass enclosure as well as a tennis ball. Dr. J placed the tennis ball in the center of the table, then he put the clear glass over it. He then started the video recording equipment.

Dr. J explained, "Matt, has been able to move items using only mental concentration. And, as I had explained to you earlier, I can see on his x-rays that Matt has an unusually large Pineal gland as well as other cerebral structures. I'm not exactly sure if it's a neoplasm, plaque or some other growth. But, for right now I'd like for you to see what he can do. Matt, please have a seat."
I sat down at the table.
I sat down, "Okay."
Dr. J., "Do whatever you want."

I looked at the tennis ball under the glass enclosure. Haha! For some reason, the idea of a tennis ball under glass was humorous to me. As if the glass was a barrier, a challenge that was supposed to be difficult. I almost laughed out loud. I'm sure I was grinning. But, I remembered I was under observation. So, I relaxed and concentrated.

The ball rolled around, raised, and bounced. It bounced and stayed up. Then I made it bounce back and forth against the glass walls of the enclosure. I set it down back at the center of the table where it originally started.

Dr. Ebb, with no expression at all, pulled out a hidden notepad, pen, and started writing furiously.
After a few moments, Liz, who hadn't left the room but had watched invisibly from the back corner said out loud, "Wow..."
That startled Dr. J, and I. Dr. J turned around to Liz and said, "Thank you, Liz." Liz then left as silently as she had stayed. Dr. J then switched off the recording equipment. We noted that Dr.

Ebb had continued to write and did not talk. Dr. J. waited, and after a few moments, broke the silence and commented, "Matt came to me complaining about sleep interruptions and soon divulged his talent. We conducted some initial tests and I made an assumption that his Pineal and some other masses were... they might be connected to these abilities."
Dr. Ebb seemed not to notice and kept writing.
Dr. J continued, "Matt has commented that his sleep cycles are much better due to some recommendations I've made and that his ability has been getting easier to manage."

Dr. J and I sat for some time silently while Dr. Ebb continued to write. Then, spontaneously, he broke his writing and spoke with a voice that seemed louder than necessary. He looked up smiling and made a pronouncement so fast, that he startled both me and Dr. J with his abruptness.

Dr. Ebb, "Gentlemen, this is fascinating! I am genuinely interested in this case. Dr. Johnson, I'd like all the information you've collected so far and I'd like to get Matt into our labs to run a complete series of tests and observations. You were correct in assuming that I'd want to take an interest in his case. With our equipment and staff, there is so much we might learn. Matt, I'd like to transport you to our facilities right away. This occurrence may just be the breakthrough case that we've been preparing for."

I could see that Dr. J was thinking that he had just lost his most interesting patient, as well as, the studies, and the possibilities of pending, unrealized accolades and recognition's, yanked away with a few short minutes of note writing. I could see in his face his displeasure. He wasn't about to let his star discovery get pulled away. I could tell that he was thinking it was time for some damage control.

Dr. J said, "Dr. Ebb, It's good news to hear that you're ready to get so involved in Matt's case. I would like to stress that I am Matt's attending physician and that we have already begun a serious series of testing, observations, and lab work here, that have also been centered around Matt's schedule. We were hoping, with your help, to get some expert assistance with his physiology and on the brain masses that he has developed. We'd love to have you involved in this project and together, we can study the uniqueness of his case."

I decided I needed to add to Dr. J's argument, "Dr. Ebb, I have a work schedule that I have to keep and I'm very comfortable with Dr. Johnson and the facilities here. I'd love to have you help us out with my condition, but I am hesitant about letting other people know about... my differences. I do want to know if this is some kind of tumor. I am a little worried about the possibility of it being something bad for me."

Dr. J. followed my comment with, "I'm sure we can come up with a schedule that works for all of us and I'm confident the facilities here will be more than adequate. Should we need specialized testing, then we can make arrangements at the appropriate time and facility."
Dr. Ebb stood silent for more than a minute and made a few more scratchings on his pad. He then said, with some acknowledgment I assumed, was intended for the position that Dr. J was trying to protect, "Yes, of course. We can work with Matt, here. But, I'm certain we'll eventually need to take him to visit our facilities, when the time comes, naturally. When is the next testing scheduled? I'd like to coordinate with you on what tests have been performed. Dr. Johnson, I'd like for us to review what your plans are and make arrangements to study the growths that are present in your x-rays. I'll have my office contact you to make the appropriate arrangements. I'll need to receive full copies of your current work and findings. I am appreciative that you brought me in on his case. I look forward to working with the two of you. Now, I've got other appointments to keep today. This has been a very interesting meeting. Excellent meeting

you Matt. Have a good day gentlemen!"

With as much measure and purpose as his arrival, he exited the room. Dr. J and I were left standing in the testing room.

Me, "Dr. J. He certainly seemed... professional."
Dr. J., "Yes, he went straight to business. He doesn't seem to waste time or make any wasted movements. I wonder if he has any trouble sleeping at night! Hahaha!"
I laughed at Dr. J.'s joke. But, to myself, I wondered if Dr. Ebb would be warming up to the two of us anytime soon.

As usual, I passed Liz on the way out of Dr. J's office. "Matt," she chimed, "Remember, we're going out to Rock Taco bar and restaurant. You need to come!"
"Sounds great Liz! I'll see if Cindy is free to go." I said as I walked out the door. Without even looking back I could tell that Liz had a frown on her face. I was grinning to myself.

CHAPTER 22

The Breakup

Recently, Cindy had been busy at work as she had been put on the evening schedule for the past couple of weeks. So, we hadn't gotten together in the evenings as much as we had as when her day schedule permitted. This evening, however, was better as she had been put back on weekdays and we could now plan our evenings with some regularity. It was a beautiful day outside, so I called her at work with the idea it would be nice to enjoy the warmth and sunshine of the day with a nice cookout on the patio at home.

Cindy came over after work and began to verbally download all her day's activities. As well as all the current gossip about her fellow hospital workers. I poured her a glass of wine, and as she talked, I started to cook. She began with how the orderlies and room attendants didn't do what they are supposed to and other random gripes. Then she started telling me the juicy gossip about who couldn't stand whom and which nurse, doctor, technician, etc. had a crush on the other. "The "really important stuff," to her I was thinking to myself. However, I really couldn't have cared less.

As I had come to realize, this is a glimpse into the world of women. First, they seem to need, or maybe actually do, talk more than men. I can only assume it comes through as a natural matter of evolution. My thought about the word count discrepancy is that, for countless centuries, women have sat

by the campfire waiting for the men to come back from their hunting trips. And, while the men were away, the women spent their time tending children, foraging food, and probably, most importantly, talking with other women. Talking and waiting. The men, however, trekked through the woods or across the Savanna, quietly. Quietly stalking
prey. Men quiet, women talking. There it is, the way it was done for thousands, maybe hundreds of thousands of years. Although it may have not been done for centuries, it's probably ingrained in women almost like instinct.

The women, as I can rationalize, must have been extremely nervous while the men were away. After all, there was a lot to worry about back then. When would the men return? Would they have a successful hunt and keep everyone from starving? Would they return at all? Get lost? Get injured? Would a rival tribe come and attack while they were away? All this meant life or death, for some or all. Wow! These women had a whole lot to be concerned about. So, I give them their worry, their need to chat, their uncertainty of the future. They've earned it. It's their means of coping with the stresses of life. They talk it out.

But, I also believe this is why they've been programmed throughout the ages to have, even need, that emotional stress that they've evolved with. They need that constant emotional up-and-down to create, or maybe use up, the hormones or stresses pulsing through their bodies. And, if that emotional roller-coaster doesn't happen on its own, then they'll create it. I wonder, why does it seem that women seem to need to express their feelings? Why do they have girl bonding sessions where they cry with other women? Why do they enjoy the cheesy dramas in soap operas and chick flick movies? They must be seeking or feeding off the drama, real or imagined, and it doesn't seem to matter where it comes from, they just need it.

For example, how many times do couples go out for a night-on-the-town and the end up having a minor disagreement, or even a full-blown argument? Or, possibly, a relationship disaster? Some women appear to be able to start conflict without even the slightest concern as for what, or why. "Were you looking at that girl? Is so-and-so prettier than me? Do you still love me?" The "trap" questions happen. And to us guys, it comes from nowhere, out of the blue.

We guys think everything is going smoothly. We're happy, mostly. But now, we have questions to answer. And some, although they may try their best, don't escape. "Why do you want to know what I think about such-and-such? What do you want me to say? Where are you going with this?" The smarter guys may even try; "Oh baby, you're the only girl for me. You know I love you." We may analyze and guess, but for our life, we don't know where the questions are coming from, or where they're going. The best of us try to dodge, ignore, or redirect. Or, say what we think needs to be said. The unlucky guys, they get dragged in. Endless interrogation. No right answer. An unhappy mate and a spoiled night. I pity and feel for the unprepared and the witless man. But for the emotional woman, they must create their tension. It's the woman's insecurity instinct. And, one way or another, they're going to talk their way through it.

Cindy, as I had gotten to know, had the curious habit of talking about work, or traffic, or shopping, clothes, workmates... or whatever she had on her mind as soon as we'd meet up after being apart. Her usual practice was that, for 15, 20, even 30 minutes, she'd talk about anything and everything. I'd listen, briefly comment or acknowledge with an "Oh wow" or "Really" or "Incredible." Just enough to let her know I was almost paying attention. Then, when the appropriate amount of time had passed, or her internal word limit was reached, and with a seemingly abrupt conclusion she'd say, "OK, I'm done." She'd throw her hands up, slap her thighs, smile, and that would be it. She'd stop talking.

The constant stream of words would end. Her download was

complete. She could now listen to me or go on to do something else. It would amuse me every time that she'd stop like this. Her word quota would be reached or her information supply was transmitted and that was it. She'd be done. She would be verbally satisfied. I think she also was aware that she needed this. That is probably why she would always throw her hands up and slap her thighs and then say, "Ok, I'm done!". It was always a bit funny, and we'd both laugh.

That same scene was happening again this early evening. With a glass of wine in hand, she sat on the sofa and told me about her day. Meanwhile, I got things ready in the kitchen while going back and forth cooking out on the sunny patio. I made my way between the kitchen, through the family room, and out to the grill and back as she told me her day. After a while, on one of my trips to the patio, I noticed she had stopped talking. She had fallen asleep. Head tilted back, her back in the corner of the sofa, with the wine glass in her hand just tipping to the point of spilling. I took the glass from her hand and sat it on the new coffee table. I decided to let her sleep as apparently, she must have had a hard day. She never got to the "OK, I'm done" moment.

Deciding to let her sleep, I finished up the cooking, grabbed her wine glass, and sat in the chair across from her. Not wanting to waste any wine, I drank the last of it from her glass. Before I knew it, I too was fast asleep.

I woke with a jerk and with that familiar falling feeling that I've have had numerous times in my life. As I woke I looked around the room. I had the magicians glasses on as I had been using them this sunny day as sunglasses. I looked over at Cindy, and there above her head was a purple haze with some moving pictures in it. As I watched, the fog around her head was already starting to dissipate. But, in the fog, I could see Cindy talking with a man, a man dressed as a doctor A dark-haired, handsome, good looking doctor. Then, as I watched, I saw sex. She was having sex. Her head was tilting back, her back was arching, bare legs were shaking. There was no sound but I could see her moaning. Naked bodies were moving together. Then I saw the face of a man. A man I've never seen before. Worse yet, that man wasn't me. The fog disappeared with the last image I saw being of that man's face.

"What's this?" I thought to myself. "Is Cindy having sex with another guy, a doctor?" My mind started racing. Is this vision stuff real? Can it be? I felt like I had just opened a door and witnessed Cindy naked, in bed with another man. Is that why she had been working lots of odd hours? Nights and evenings? I was getting furious. "What is this image? What the fricking hell is she remembering? When did this take place? I took off the glasses and stood up. Cindy woke to the sound of my moving around.

"Hey, babe" she drowsily spoke. "Did I fall asleep?" I didn't know what to say. The image of her having sex with another man was fresh in my head. I had a flood of emotions running through my mind. My mind jumped from thought to thought. I thought we were doing so well. Who was this guy? She could tell that I was agitated and she asked, "What's going on babe? Is dinner ready?" I answered, "Yeah, dinner is ready." I went to the kitchen to get our plates.

She said, "You didn't burn it or anything?" I plopped the plates on the table as she walked towards it.

I answered her again, "Nope, not burned. But I have some questions for you. First, where have you been the past several evenings and nights?"

She said, "Working."

I fumbled for words I was so furious, "I thought you and I was... we were... we've been getting on so well. I thought we were a good pair. I thought you cared about me, about us." I added angrily.

She said, "I do, what's going on? I've been at work. I told you. Don't you know where I've been?"

The kettle in my head was starting to boil over. My thoughts were confused but also on fire. The thought of her cheating on me was pumping up my adrenaline. I felt nothing but anger towards her as the vision of her having sex with another man kept flowing through my head.

I started yelling at her, "I know you've been cheating on me and I'm not going to take another minute of it. And screw you, I'm not making dinner for some whore!" I slid my arm across the table and wiped the plates of food to the floor.

She stood up, responded, "I don't know what the fuck you're talking about. Who told you this? But never mind, and you know what? You can go screw yourself. You're an ass and I haven't done anything wrong. So, fuck off. I'm tired and I'm going home." She grabbed her purse and with a final "fuck you" and a door slam she left. I was too upset to clean up the mess. I grabbed a bottle of scotch, a glass and some ice and poured a big shot, then another. The thought of her sleeping with some guy was infuriating. Women are such fuckers. Always looking to trade up for some dude that has more.

More money, more looks, more status, more dick, more... whatever. Go fuck them. After a couple of hours of fuming and cussing, the Scotch did its job. I fell asleep.

CHAPTER 23

Boys Night Out

The next day I called Mike and told him what happened. "Wow, dude. It looks like you got screwed. Too bad shit like this happens." He said, "We need to go out, just us guys. Like we used to. You need to get your mind off things." We made plans to go to a bar/restaurant that evening after work. So we did. I met Mike at the bar and we ordered drinks and appetizers. We talked about girls, girlfriends, past failures, past glorious fucks, and why women are inevitably always a disappointment. And as we talked, we drank.

As fate would have it, right when the thought of having anything to do with women at all was revolting, who should walk up to the bar? None other than the tall, over blond, bright red lipstick wearing Liz. And, as always, wearing a giant smile and another short miniskirt to match. " OH WOW, Matt! I didn't think you were going to come." She slid up next to me and put her hand on mine and squeezed. I had totally forgotten Liz had said she was coming here, this

night, this place. "I'm so glad you came out, and I see you brought your friend with you again. It seems like you guys go out together by yourselves quite a bit. Just two guys out all alone? Are you two out trying to meet girls...?" She laughed loudly. "And I'm sorry, I forgot your name." "Mike." Mike said, "Mike, from the party." Mike shook her hand. "Oh yeah, I remember. Let me go tell my friends I'm over here." And with that, she bounded off.

"Wow dude, I think that girl really wants your D." Mike grinned. "You know she's coming back," I said to Mike. Mike said, "Yep, and I'm going to leave you here to fend for yourself. After all, I told Phyllis that I'd meet her later. And guess what? It's later." "Oh, you can be such a dick," I smirked at Mike. "You know I don't want to sit here and talk with her," I told him. Mike said, "I know. But go ahead and chat with her awhile. Why not? It'll help you forget about Cindy, at least for a little while." "Mike, you really do know how to be a pecker-head, and thanks for bringing her up, you dick. But really, Mike, thanks for getting me out. Now, go on, get the hell out of here. I can take care of myself." Mike left saying, "OK big dog. Give me a call tomorrow, I want to hear about everything!" "OK, tell Phyllis I said hi." He said, "Will do," and he made for the exit.

Liz returned and took Mike's empty seat. We ordered a round of Martinis and Liz asked, "So where did Mike take off to? Did he leave you here all alone? Where's your other half, Cindy?" I told Liz, "Mike, he had to meet his girl. Cindy, she and I, well, we're having a rough patch."
"Really? What's going on with you guys? I thought you two were tight. Does that mean you're available to ask me out soon?" She asked. I could tell she was surprised and her female mind was working overtime with internal questions. Meanwhile, I was thinking, "Gawd, this girl has no boundaries." But, I did admire that she didn't have any problem saying what she wants. "How's your girl's night-out going?" I asked her. "Good," she said. "But, I can hang out with them anytime."

We sat and talked and she turned out to be super fun. An energetic and funny girl. It was great to have the distraction, the flirty talk, the extra drinks. And, I liked the attention. Eventually, it was getting late and I was thinking it was a good time to go home. I looked at my phone. No texts, no calls. No contact from Cindy at all. I imagined she went to go play doctor, with the doctor.

Liz saw that I was looking down at my phone. "Hey, no calls from Cindy?" "Nope," I said. I could tell she was happy to say that. But then she said with complete sincerity, "I hope everything works out with you two. I hate to hear when people break-up." I was so surprised to hear her say that. Maybe Liz wasn't as self-absorbed as I thought she was. It was time to go so I told her, "I've got to go. Thanks for hanging out with me Liz. It was fun talking with you. I'll talk to you soon." "You too." She said, "Call me anytime if you want to hang out again." I went home and fell right to sleep on the couch. It was a good thing to have gone out tonight, I thought. Although, once home, I was already missing my sleeping partner.

CHAPTER 24

The Professionals

The doctors had scheduled another meeting. We met at Dr. J's office but now the meeting had a new feel to it. Dr. Ebb had made several changes to Dr. J.'s testing procedures. It seemed like we were starting all over again. First, they had me perform a full physical. Then, a full range of tests, blood tests, eye exams, heart and stress test, urine and stool samples, prostrate exam, many of the same tests that Dr. J had me do, but even more, and more thorough. It seemed like they had me do every test imaginable. Also, several more X-rays. Most of them were of my head. However, I insisted that they didn't put me anywhere near an MRI machine. Dr. J had to explain the previous bad reaction to Dr. Ebb.

At some point between examinations, I asked why all the new tests, and why were they doing some duplicates of previous tests. Dr. J. explained that he and Dr. Ebb decided it was a good idea to follow a set of procedures that Dr. Ebb suggested. He was very thorough in explaining that we needed a full range of information to establish baselines. Something to measure or go back to and compare should anything change. Dr. J was working well with Dr. Ebb and as soon as one test was completed, another test was already ready.

I found it interesting that they didn't seem to want to see any of my floating tricks. I can only suppose that they were proceeding scientifically. One step at a time. It took the entire day and it was rather exhausting. Finally, they were finished and it was already started to get dark outside. I was happy that the tests were done and while we were concluding, I had a thought. As Dr. J and Dr. Ebb stood near me talking about the tests, saying their goodbyes and thanking me for being such a good patient, I saw a pen, an expensive, very nice pen in Dr. Ebb's breast shirt pocket. I said, "Gentlemen, one moment." I raised my hands to them to have them stop and take notice. We three stood in silence for a few seconds as I relaxed and closed my eyes. I said a mini mantra, "Mind... Shift..." to myself and then, using only my thoughts, felt the pen in his pocket. I lifted the pen from his shirt. I squinted my eyes open just enough to see it move and center between the three of us. I spun it around in the air a few times then slowly moved it back towards Dr. Ebb. He reached out with his hand and took it from the air. " There you are doctors, a reminder of why we're here. And, also, that I'm still able to do it!" We all three laughed a bit. I realized that after today, they were probably just as exhausted as I was.

On the way out, at the front desk, I saw Liz. She was talking to a man in a black suit and shiny black shoes who looked like he probably used the same military hairstylist as Dr. Ebb. "Wow, you're here kind of late," I said to her as she signed me out for the day-long visit. She said "Yep, they asked me to stay late and do some filing, and some other stuff. There are these test evaluations that need to be organized right away, like tonight. They're keeping me really busy. Some kind of important stuff going on, I think. So, here I am. I did see you on the roster. I was hoping you'd stop by and say hi. You're here kind of late yourself aren't you?" I said, "Yes, a long day. Can't wait to get home. Oh, by-the-way, thanks for hanging out with me the other evening. I was feeling rather down." "Hey, I understand." She said, "Everybody goes through these things. How is it with you two? Any contact yet? Did you and her sort it all out yet?" "Well, no. I haven't heard a thing." I told her, "I mean, it's a tough subject to bring up. I get angry too fast. And I probably don't want to know any details about it. It still gets me so mad."

"Well if you'd like, I can meet you in a little while. You know, get a drink somewhere. We can wind down a bit. You can tell me your frustrations, I'll listen." she said smiling.

"Ah, thanks Liz, but I'm pretty pooped. Thanks for being a friend. Don't work too late. With that, I turned to leave. As I started walking I thought to myself, "Why not have a quick drink with her? She's harmless and I did enjoy talking to her quite a bit the other evening." So, with that thought, I turned around and went back to tell her that I changed my mind.

When I turned around, I approached the man in the suit from behind. I noticed that he had the sign-in clipboard in his hands and with a large black pen was blacking out some sign-in/out times. "Hey, Liz," I said. The suited man was startled from my approach and without speaking at all, he gave the clipboard back to Liz and walked off. "I think I'll take you up on that drink. Is Keegan's bar good? It's close and my bartender buddy Shawn is the new owner." "Sure, give me a little bit and I'll see you there. You might even talk me into having two martini's." She smiled. "OK, I'll see you in a little bit," I told her.

I walked out thinking about how the suited man wiped my visit off the roster. Hum, I think maybe Dr. J and Dr. Ebb are keeping this testing a secret. They probably don't want their work leaking out. At least until they have some findings. Or, an odd uncomfortable thought crossed my mind, "Or maybe, if they screw something up." Everything these days has to be taken in a CYA (Cover Your Ass) context with liabilities and lawsuits being thrown around all the time, especially in the medical field. It's like any mistake at all and some idiot thinks they've won the lottery. Sue, sue, sue! What a hindrance to medicine. And, to business in general. Hopefully, that wasn't going to be the case and I made a mental note to ask Dr. J about the suited guy during my next visit.

Liz met me at the bar. We talked and eventually had more than one martini. Unfortunately, this evening the company had a worse outcome. And, it wasn't Liz's fault. We had a good talk about things in general but not about anything important or anything about relationships. I guess, for at that time, it was a good thing to not talk about anything stressful or upsetting. It was relaxing. She had a different look to her than she did when she was dressed to go out. I thought her reduced amount of makeup and lipstick made her look a little better, a bit more "housewifey," maybe a little more like girlfriend material. She smiled and laughed as she always does and eventually I found myself sitting rather close to her. After a while, she had turned and was chatting with Shawn behind the bar as he was busy try-ing to tidy up. It was starting to get late. I noticed how blond and shiny her hair looked next to the smooth skin of her neck. I could smell the essence of the perfume on her hair
along with the faint smell of a day-long immersion of antiseptic hospital air. As she turned her attention back to me, she was very close. I leaned in and kissed her.

I sat back. "Wow," I said out loud. "I think I shouldn't have done that." "That's OK," she said with a sly smile. "I was kind of look-ing forward to it. But I think you may be missing somebody, and it's getting to be too late for me to be out on a "school night." I chuckled and said, "You're probably right. I think it's time to go home." It was right then that Shawn behind the bar slid my bill across the counter, perfect timing I thought. After paying the bill and as we got up to leave, I said thanks and gave her a good-night hug. I was thinking she's a better, more in-tuned girl than I had originally passed judgment on. I respected that she could sense where I was emotionally. Hell, my current disappoint-ment with Cindy probably showed on me more than I realized. I went home, feeling more alone than ever. Cindy was on my mind. I wanted to talk to her, be with her again. I almost gave her a call, but a drunken, tired, desperate-sounding booty call wasn't going to impress her or patch things up. It might make matters even worse. I might blow up angry again. Or, become a blubbering mass of spineless man jello. Who knows? I'm just tired. So home I went. Tired and sad. It was no wonder that I had no problem falling asleep.

CHAPTER 25

The Re-Connect

Now that I was home alone in the evening, trying not to think about Cindy, I had begun to ponder more about the times when I was able to see the "thought's" that I had seen. As I recalled in those instances, the first thing I realized was, is that I had no control over when, or where, or how it happened. It had only happened twice. That's not a very long track record to begin to make assumptions. Both times I saw visions, I was tired, drowsy, and I had to have the magician's glasses on to see it. I wondered if it had happened before. How many times before? Without the magician's glasses on, I wouldn't have known a thing. Who knows how many thoughts I would have seen if I had had the glasses and if the conditions were right. I wondered if there was a way to see thoughts when I wanted to see them.

And then I thought about the levitating and the moving of things at night. Now that I think about it, not just at night but when I've been sleeping. The crashing vase, things that had moved, Cindy floating off the bed. Those thoughts made me shudder. All those past years when things were out-of-place or when bumps were heard in the night. These scenarios were beginning to feel a little scary. What if I can't control what happens to people or things? Could I accidentally damage something? Like, start a fire or even worse, maybe hurt somebody? Then what? Would I have to go live somewhere remote like a hermit? Maybe in a cave? Or, on an island somewhere? An island? At least that sounds a little better. Ha!

On the other hand, if the visions and floating of things are related, then I got some comfort in that I could do these floating tricks on command, while I was awake. At least then, I was in control. I had also found, as I practiced, some words to recite that helped get me directly into a frame of mind to relax and concentrate. To help get the feeling, I would calm myself and say internally, "Mind... shift, mind.... shift, mind... shift." Saying that to myself became a quick way to immerse me into a trance-like calmness that blocked out worldly distractions. "Mind shift" was my self-made trigger to bring me inside myself.

I was proud I had learned what I had learned. I could control these abilities during the day. But, these thoughts that I couldn't control at night, or when asleep, that was still a concern. It was the idea of not having any control that was worrying me. I decided that I should let Dr. J and Dr. Ebb know what my thoughts and worries were. Maybe they'd have some ideas.

It had been several days since my "disagreement" with Cindy and I decided to send her a text. No matter what the current situation was, it would be better for all if we cleared the air or closed on good terms. All I wanted was to have things back to the way they were. Cindy and I going out or staying in. She and I, having fun. I was missing our little heated conversations, our mini disagreements, opposing opinions, as well as our shared likes and similar experiences. Sharing our life stories. I even missed her after work "verbal downloads." She was a firecracker at times, and I missed it. It's those things, after all, that give companionship a bit of spice as well as familiarity. And the sex. Oh Gawd, Yes... the sex. Even if everything else was off relationship-wise, I'd still be missing the great, satisfying sex. I was wondering if she felt the same. I was longing to feel that cute feminine body.

My text went, "Cindy, I apologize for losing my cool. That's not what I meant to do. My emotions got the best of me and for that, I'm sorry." That was it. I didn't want to write the tons of thoughts and things I wanted to say. Better to say I was sorry, accept, and move on if that was going to be the case. I was reaching out without forcing explanations or implying faults. My mind went blank after I sent the text.

She responded within a few minutes with... "Hi." Only, "Hi?" "I thought, that's it? "Hi?" Nothing but, "Hi?" What am I suppose to do with that?" Then a few agonizing minutes later she texted again. "About time you texted me. What are you up to?" I knew her well enough to know that, just by her question, she was giving me a chance to ask her out. At least I was pretty sure. "Would you like to have a drink with me at Keegan's later?" I texted. I was so nervous when I asked. "Feels like a first date," I thought in that instant. "Sure," she replied, "what time?" "8:00 good?" Her, "Ok, see you at 8." Short texts, but good results. All I wanted to do was to blast out, all at once, all that I was thinking. Damn it! I need to calm myself. I need to get myself organized. Maybe at the bar, I could get some questions answered. I was apprehensive about talking to her, seeing her. Would she want to get back together? Was she seeing a doctor? She had been the only thing on my mind since that dinner. I had a continuous stream of thoughts about her, tons of different questions, things I wanted to say, and questions to get her answers on. I was torn between wanting her and knowing this could be the end of it all. I was happy and yet worried to meet her, all at the same time.

When evening came, I knew I wanted to make a good show of myself. I needed to look good and stand firm, confident, and show her I wasn't phased by her absence. And, I wanted to look like an attractive male, a man with options. So, I wore a sharp looking brown sport coat with a lite blue button-down shirt (blue brings out the color of my blue eyes,) my best fitting pair of jeans, a belt that matched my light brown cowboy boots. These boots have a great shape to them and fancy stitching as well. But, the best part is, they make me stand about two inches taller, which is always a plus - gals love a tall guy! I was ready. Looking good, feeling good, standing tall, an attractive, confident man, I thought to myself. I'm ready, now, off to the bar. I showed up a little early hoping to get a preferred seat and maybe a relaxing starter drink. Shawn sat me right down.

As soon as I had my drink I couldn't stop alternating between staring at the entrance and drinking my drink a little too fast. Finally, Cindy came in ten minutes late, which was just enough to make me a bit more nervous. She looked, well, fantastic. Better than fantastic. She was dressed nice! I mean sexy, very sexy! I thought, way too sexy for an Irish pub. My first thought was she was doing the same as me, trying to sell the merchandise and working the "look good" angle. The short dress she wore was tight-fitting and hugged her butt and thighs and made the most of her medium-sized but ample bust. I always thought she had an excellent body and this dress showed it off. The dress was tight-fitting and colorful. And, it exuded femininity and sexuality at the same time. But, my favorite part was the low, low cut back that started from the bottom of her waist just barely above her butt and reached up to her neckline where it hung from the edges of both shoulders. Acres of soft skin and neck, waist, and shoulder blades. I loved seeing those shoulder blades and the valley of flawless skin in-between. It was a smooth curve that begged for a light touch, my light touch. The side view of her dress was an artful curve along her waist and made your eyes look for the cup of her breasts that seemed to want to play peek-a-boo from underneath the material. Incredibly teasing to the male eye. Wow! I thought to myself, I've already lost this battle.

She sat down.
"Hi, Matt how are you?"
"Good, good. How are you doing?"
"Great, she said, been very busy with work. Although, sometimes I hang with my girlfriends."

"Yep, me too."

The thought of Liz popped into my head and I had a claustrophobic guilty moment with the thought that I wouldn't want Cindy to know that I'd been out, but not out, with another gal. The idea of me cheating wasn't where my mind needed to be at this moment. I needed to focus on her. Thankfully, Shawn interrupted at that moment to get us some drinks. I immediately came back to concentrate on Cindy.

Me, "I've been getting thoroughly worked over at the sleep clinic by Dr. Ebb and Dr. J."
Cindy, "Wow, have they found out anything?"
Me, "No, but according to them, they're just getting started. They have to get baselines or beginning data or something. I think the real tests are going to start soon."
"Well, that's good." She said.

Whew, so far, so good, I was thinking to myself. She seems open, interested. Not angry or anything.

"Yes, I think so." I continued, "I will tell you, I'm still a little worried that I may have something wrong with me. Possibly something bad in the long run."

Geez, I thought, That sounds so depressing.

"Well, I certainly hope its not that." She answered. "Are you still able to do... stuff?"
"Yes." I replied, "And there's something that I haven't told you. And, it's something I probably should have told you before. I guess now, now seems like a good time to tell you." I surprised myself that this topic came up so fast. I guess it was the only thing on my mind.
'OK, what is it?" She was curious, but I could sense that she was bracing for some really bad news.
"Well, with Mike's magician's glasses on, right after I wake up from a bad dream, a dream where I feel like I'm falling. I think I

can see memories."

"What? I don't understand," she questioned.

"A while back, at Chuck and Kathy's party, the one you were working late and couldn't make it, I fell asleep on a sofa and woke up abruptly with a falling sensation. I was wearing Mike's magician's glasses because I was tired and didn't want anyone to see that I was taking a quick nap. But, after I had startled myself awake when I looked around, I saw some thoughts that, I think, were thoughts that this woman was having. They were there, like a small video, visions in the air by her head. I could see them

as she was telling a story. I could see it. I could see what she was thinking almost as clear as I see you sitting here. I couldn't believe my eyes. It didn't last long and then faded away."

Cindy, "You've got to be kidding. Who was this woman?"

"Oh, nobody that I knew," I told her. "We were introduced during the evening but I can't recall her name."

Cindy, "And did you see anyone else's thoughts? Or just hers?" Cindy began squinting her eyes a little bit. I don't think she even knew she was doing it.

Me, "It was only her, and she was with some guy."

Cindy, "Only her, just hers? Why her? Was she pretty?" I could sense Cindy's jealousy.

Me, "She... she didn't look bad." I was thinking she was pretty damn hot, but I knew better than to feed that tiger at this point. I continued, "But, I think I know how I saw her thoughts, and I'm pretty sure that it's somehow related to my levitation tricks."

Cindy, "Well that's interesting. Interesting that you can see this one girl's thoughts. Did you tell her?"

Me, "No! No, nothing like that. I didn't say a thing. It only happened once, at that time. But, (I hesitated a moment,) there is this other time this happened. I began to feel a little bit of anger and a little bit of fear that this was finally coming up. "The night I got so angry, at you, it happened then too."

"What?" She remarked.

I reluctantly began to tell her, "You were asleep on the couch and I had drifted off to sleep myself. When I woke up, I saw you sleeping, and I think you may have been dreaming. I could see, in this weird fog around your head, it looked like, like you were having sex with another man."

Cindy, "I was having sex with another man! Another man? Who?"

Me, "A dark-haired man. A doctor, I think."

Cindy, "So, you THINK you saw me having sex with another man? While I was sleeping? And you THINK, I was dreaming of having sex with someone, and you got mad, mad about that?"

Me, "Um, yeah. Pretty much."

Cindy, "Wow, that's pathetic. You have got to be kidding me."

Me, "No, it's not pathetic. After all, I had seen the other woman's story as she was telling it. And I felt that it was true. I could see what she was describing."

Cindy, "OK, so, go back. I'm asleep and you think you see me having sex. And you think it's real?, And maybe, MAYBE, it was a dream?"

Me, "Yeah, I guess that's it."

All of a sudden, I was feeling rather foolish.

Cindy, "I hope you should know that I haven't been with anyone else but you."

Me, "Yeah, but it seemed so real to me."

Cindy, "That might be, but I'm telling you right now, that isn't the case. That's never happened. And what the hell? Now you've got some other weird "thing" that you can do. You're unbelievable! I'm not even sure I believe it."

Me, "Well, then, why do you think you were dreaming about having sex with a doctor? Some dark-haired, handsome guy?"

Cindy, "I don't know. But if I were to guess, I'd say I might have been thinking about the new doctor that has started his residency at the hospital recently. He is good looking and I have to work with him but I've never had sex with him, or anybody else for that matter. Not since I've been with you."

Me, "Really?"

Cindy, "Really..."

Me, "Well, it seemed so real."

Cindy, "Nope, never happened. And also, he's happily married. He talks about his wife all the time. Anyway, maybe I was dreaming about sex. And, maybe dreaming about work too. But dreams, only dreams. And I don't know how dreams work. They just happen."

Me, "Yeah, wow. Ok, you're right. I didn't see the two of you to-gether in my vision. I probably assumed too much, too fast. I'm sorry I blew up at you."

Cindy, "You should be."

"I've missed you," I said quietly.

Cindy said, "I've missed you too. But, not the asshole you."

We both laughed a bit. Then Shawn, as secretly attentive and professional as always, sat down another round of drinks and an appetizer "on-the-house." We drank and snacked and chatted. We went home soon after to enjoy each other's company and to dive into each other's sex-deprived bodies.

The backless dress was the most seductive thing to take off that I've ever had the pleasure to remove off a woman. My hands did get the chance to move slowly across that smooth silky skin, between her shoulders and down to her backside, up, down, over and over. She hummed a soft moan as I touched her as delicately as I could. Soft, like a breath of air pushing a piece of down across a marble table. We ended up slowly escalating our built-up passions late into the night. After our bodies had been satisfied with the exertions of our re-connection, we both fell into a deep, contented sleep.

CHAPTER 26

The Gift

The next morning we both woke up and I noticed we both had big smiles as we got ready for work. As we left the house, we happened to notice two identical gray vans in the street across from the house. I usually make a habit of checking on vehicles in my neighborhood as I like to keep track of who comes and goes. Kind of like an unofficial neighborhood watch thing. I like to think my neighbors do the same thing too. On occasion, it seems that the neighbors seem to know everybody's comings and goings, which, overall, can be kind of a good thing. However, these two vans stood out, first, because they were the same make and color, also, because they had "GV" before a number on the license plates. "GV," I thought, that's government vehicles. So, that's a bit of a relief. Little to worry about there. Most likely not burglars waiting to clean out my house of TV's and loose jewelry. But, then again, the question is, "what are government vehicles doing here?" I commented to Cindy, "Hey, did you notice the two government cars there?" She said, "Yeah, looks like it. Maybe they are tapping houses to find out who might be a terrorist." "Yep" I laughed. "Or maybe it's the new neighbor and some of his work buddies?" We had a long goodbye kiss and made plans to have dinner later. She was looking particularly cute in her nurses' uniform before she drove away.

I met with my work crew that morning and sent them on their route. I had scheduled an afternoon visit with the doctors again at Dr. J's office at the hospital. As I walked in, I saw the same suit-wearing guy that was there during my last visit. But this time, he was stationed right in front of the examination room where we had done our previous "baseline testing." I stepped inside the room and saw that the doctors were ready to do some serious testing. There was not one, but several cameras set up, and microphones, and lighting systems, and all kinds of equipment. It looked more like a movie studio setup than an examination room.

Right away I sat down with Dr. Ebb and Dr. J.

"How are you feeling Matt?" Dr. J asked.
"Great," I said, "I'm feeling as good as I've ever felt."
"Good, Good. That's great. And sleeping well?" Asked Dr. J.
"Yes, I have been sleeping great. And when I practice my "thing" I can get to sleep as fast as ever. And stay asleep too."
"Good, good." Dr. J replied.
Dr. Ebb. "Any more videos you have from odd things happening at home?"
"No. nothing," I answered.
"So, no videos at all?" Asked Dr. Ebb.
"Nope," I answered.
"Have you been floating or moving anything in public?" Dr. Ebb asked.
"No, not really. Nothing more than an occasional magic trick." I told him.
"In the bars, or at work? You haven't performed any levitations?" Ebb queried.
"Yep, pretty much. And definitely not while I'm working. But sometimes while I'm out, I'll do a card trick or two. But, even that, not as much as I used too." I answered.
"Good, good." Dr. Ebb replied.

Then Dr. Ebb proceeded to talk to me about the previous testing session.

"Well, the report from all our testing is, that you're a pretty healthy guy. We didn't find anything outside your brain that was abnormal or that would raise any concerns. Your blood work didn't bring up any issues that we need to address. And, you will be happy to know that there were no cancer markers present. However, there are some irregularities in your Melatonin production and a few other hormones we'd like to keep track of. And, in the future, we'd like for you to monitor your diet as we move forward. Also, there are some vitamins and supplemental minerals that we want to suggest. In that light, we've made a list of desirable foods that we'd like you to choose from that will help you bring up those deficient levels. Or, you can take some supplements, or both, your preference."

"And we suggest that we want you to cut down on your alcohol intake. It's bad for counting sheep," Dr. J added.

That brought a laugh from both Dr. J and myself but Dr. Ebb made no notice.

Dr. Ebb continued, "Moreover, most importantly, we think it's a good time that we start exploring the manipulations you can do, and study the structures inside your brain. The spread of internal pictures we took has us more intrigued than ever. There's something unique going on in your head with these masses. Now that we've explained the good news, it's time we try to see if any external detractors may influence your special gifts."

"Wow, gift?" That was an odd thing to hear. I'd never considered that these "tricks" I could do as a "gift." It has been a curiosity, a question, maybe even a concern or something to worry about. But, a "gift?" I let that thought sit in the back of my head as we began our next testing session.

For the next couple of hours, the doctors had me levitate a couple of different objects. However, most of the time, they instructed me to lift one of my lite hollow magician's balls. The ball was easy for me to lift, but during these lifting trials, they did all kinds of distractions. They'd flash lights in my face at

different speeds, play music or sound different tones to see if there were any effects. They also had me smell different scents and aromas. They even misted water around
me. I thought some of it was a whole lot of silly. But upon further reflection, I figured that they may have been ruling out the possibility of outside influences. For the most part, I had no problem keeping the ball levitated as long as my concentration wasn't significantly distracted. Although, sometimes it was and I did drop the ball a few times. Thankfully the tests didn't take more than a couple of hours. I was looking forward to my date with Cindy.

As the session ended I asked the doctors about the suited man at the nurses counter. Dr. Ebb spoke up, "Well, let me inform you about that. Matt, I want to let you know that I've worked with a couple of government agencies on special projects over the past several years. There are particulars in your case that would be of great interest to some of these projects. I've had some inquiries about your case since and since your situation is somewhat unique, they've asked if they can monitor our progress as we proceed in our testing. They've also expressed an interest in helping to keep your identity as "low profile" as possible, as other less desirable parties may possibly want to interfere. So, along those lines, they've stationed security personnel here. If just to help keep our information confidential, it will help us keep you safe as well as protecting our testing. You want to remain somewhat anonymous during all this, don't you?"

"Um, yes. But, a security guard? Is that necessary?" I asked.

This time Dr. J spoke up, "I think it's a good idea too. After all, can you imagine what might happen should some irrational people spread the word about how you can move objects? I can only wonder what you'd be subjected to if the general public found out. You might be in danger, some danger that we can't predict. As I see it, the security officer is here to help keep us, and you, out of harm's way. So I, for one, appreciate the enhanced security. At least for the duration of our evaluations."

"Well Ok then." I said, "That seems like good reasoning." I was thinking to myself about the reaction that Phyllis had at our dinner party. She had been scared. And, for reasons that I didn't quite understand. I didn't see how any of this would be a threat to her. Yet, she was "put off" by it. I agreed with them, "I can certainly see the need to keep this confidential. This is something I hadn't considered necessary, but I'm on-board with it."

"That's great," they replied. "So, we'll keep proceeding into your case, and we'll see you at our next meeting. And," Dr. Ebb added, "For our and your security, I think it'd be a good idea if you'd refrain from demonstrating any levitation's in public." I said, "Ok, will do." And on that note, it was time to go meet Cindy.

CHAPTER 27

Something to Follow

Cindy, Mike and Phyllis and I decided to meet up for an evening out. We met at Keegans Pub for dinner and drinks and I was feeling great about life in general. Cindy and I were on the mend, my medical report overall was great, and I was working towards finding out some answers about my "condition." While we were having dinner, it was nice to hear everyone talking, laughing, and getting caught up on everybody's goings-on. I told Mike and Phyllis what was happening with me and the testing at the hospital, and how the doctors seemed so interested to find out what I could do and what was happening inside my head. Mike said that he still wanted to be my manager for a "traveling show" and make some big money in the process. And, to not let those doctors, "Mess it up." He said he had big plans for flying me, then he corrected, "us," out to film an Oprah show one day, and become famous and wealthy at the same time. He mentioned how the "Oprah effect" made everyone famous just by showing up or being mentioned on her show. We finished our food and drinks and felt it was about time to call it an evening.

Mike and Phyllis said they wanted to hit a dance club for one more drink but Cindy and I were tired and felt like "chilling" at home. We said our goodbye's and went our separate ways.

On our ride home, Cindy was so tired she started to sleep in the passenger seat. As I drove, something stuck in my head that Mike said. He had made a verbal mistake of saying, "I could fly" instead of, "We could fly." That comment kept going through my mind. "Wow," I thought. "What if I could make myself fly. Fly? That would be incredible! Maybe? Possibly? Haha, No? But, why not?" After all, we had caught, on video, Cindy floating in the bedroom. Something had made her float. And, there was the night when Cindy saw me floating above the bed, and we had the video of that too. Had I made myself float? The thought made me curious. "Maybe I should try it. What could it hurt?"

When we got home, Cindy went straight to bed. I popped a beer from the fridge then went into the living room and decided to practice levitating one of my magician's balls. I floated the ball over the table for a minute or two. I made it float so close that I could see my distorted face in its reflective surface. I moved the ball back to the center of the coffee table, then took a drink of beer and sat back on the sofa. Then, I thought, "Well, here I am. Let's see how it goes. I want to see if I can do the same thing to myself." I went to the center of the living room floor and sat down. I did my calming chant and decided to lay back on the floor. I closed my eyes and visualized myself rising off the floor. I focused on feeling the weight of my body and the flatness of the floor on my back.

Right away, I felt a wave of heat flow through my body. It took the breath out of me. It was so dis-concerning I was immediately distracted and had to start over. It took me several tries until I started to get used to the sensation and could begin to ignore it. As I tried, right at the moment when I'd start to feel lighter, just when I could sense I was about to lift off the floor, I'd begin to feel unstable. Like I was balancing on my back on a thin string with no support to hold on to. I was wobbly, like a lumberjack trying to balance on a floating log. And again, feeling out-of-balance, I'd lose concentration and hit the floor with a thud. After several tries, I rolled over on my stomach to relieve the nauseousness that I was causing myself.

"Well, this is interesting. I'm am almost able to do it, but I feel so sick that I cause myself to lose concentration and fall." As I pondered that thought, and right at that instant, I noticed I felt so much better lying on my stomach. I had my head on my hands and my face was down, staring inches to the floor. "Maybe this is better? Let's try this face-down." I relaxed and concentrated. I felt warm energy go through the middle of my body. There was hot radiation that was centered along my spine, but it spread out and enveloped me in a warm, comforting feeling throughout my entire body. It made me think of when I read about how to calm a crying baby. You place it face-down with it over your shoulder or on your knee. This must be how a baby must feel when it's being calmed by resting it stomach-down. That position is said to resemble the natural position of a fetus in the womb. It's familiar to a baby and the baby feels like it's "at home" and almost always stops crying. "Ha, now I'm the big baby."

I felt myself rise off the floor! I slowly opened my eyes to see that I was hovering a few feet above where I had been laying. I noticed I was smiling to myself. Smiling and also feeling a radiating glow that seemed to be filling everything inside my body. I floated for a few seconds then, with one movement, quickly pulled my legs up to my stomach and then stood straight up. There I stood, in the middle of the room, feeling a little dizzy from the quick twist.

Exhilaration! Incredible! Wow! I did it! Then, I felt another wave in my body, but this time it was fatigue. I was tired! That concentration took a hell of an effort. I felt a little woozy and needed to sit down. I sat on the couch pondering my feat. I was rather proud of myself, and at the same time amazed. I imagined I felt like a dad that just watched his son hit a little league baseball for the first time. Exhilarating! But, now I knew I was exhausted. As I walked to the bedroom my eyes were already closing. I went straight to bed and snuggled in close to Cindy. I fell into a deep asleep as soon as I hit the pillow.

I woke up the next morning feeling good after a great night's sleep. I put on the coffee for when Cindy would be getting up and turned on the TV to catch the morning news. As I watched, I reflected on what happened last night, "What an interesting development this is." I had to try it again. I went and laid face-down on the living room floor and began to concentrate. I felt myself rise off the floor. I stayed there, mid-air, absorbing the sensations, looking around like it was the first time I've ever entered my living room. Then, Cindy walked in. I noticed her at the doorway and with the distraction of her walking in, I lost concentration and fell to the floor.

I don't know why, but I was feeling silly and guilty at the same time. When she entered, with a bit of a startle, she stopped and said, "Oh!" I smiled at her from the floor. "Good morning sleepyhead," I said. She said, "Good morning to you too. Aaaand, What's... new?" I laughed a little and said, "I've discovered something new." "You don't say?" She responded. "You want your coffee?" I asked. She said, "Sure." I went and poured her a coffee and gave her a quick morning kiss. She sat down with her coffee and I told her about my discovery.

"Last night Mike mentioned something about "flying" somewhere. So, that gave me the idea that I might be able to float or maybe even fly, like my lifting tricks, if I tried hard enough. And, last night, I did." She said, "And this morning too, I take?" "Yeah. It felt so incredible, I decided to try it again this morning." She said, "Wow, you're something else."

I asked, "You wanna see?" She said, "Sure. Ok." I went to the center of the room and laid on the floor. I cleared my mind, forgot distractions, and started floating. It was a great feeling. I only opened my eyes slightly to help keep distractions at a minimum. I wanted to keep the "feeling" active in my body. I moved forward, then back to the center of the room. I ignored everything and thought only about where I wanted to go. I then floated myself to an upper corner of the room, turned around, then back to the center again. I twisted myself to stand upright and stood up. Now came the wave of tiredness. And, I got dizzy, so I sat down on the couch before I fell over with exhaustion.

As I sat there recovering, she commented, "That's the strangest thing you've done yet." I said, "I think you're right." "Your "visions" thing is weird but this, this takes the cake." "Yeah it does," I said, "But you know, to me, it's so very cool. It feels like something natural, almost comforting. It's like I'm in tune with the universe. And as for those visions, there's nothing I know to control that. They just come and go whenever. They seem so random. This floating though, I love it. It feels good. However, it is also so draining." She said, "Well, that's one more thing those doctors are going to have to figure out for you. Maybe soon they'll come up with an explanation." I said, "Yeah, you're right. This is one hell of a mystery. And by-the-way, I've got another appointment with those guys tomorrow. You want to meet me there at the hospital and we can head out after?" "Sure," she said, "sounds good to me."

We left together and as we left I noticed there was two grey GV plated vans in the neighborhood again. "Looks like our terrorist team is on the job again today." I said, "Sure does," Cindy commented. "I hope they are going to get whoever they're looking for today." "I do too," I said. "They're hogging up the good parking spaces!" She laughed and I gave Cindy a goodbye kiss and she left for work. To myself, I was thinking that those vans were probably Dr. Ebb's associates keeping an eye on me. I thought that it seemed a bit extreme, but as long as nobody was bothering anyone, no harm done. As an afterthought, I wondered, who was paying for all this security?

CHAPTER 28

The Incredible Story

The next day, as I arrived at the hospital for my next testing session, I saw another 2 black vans in the parking lot with GV plates. Same vehicles, just a different color. "Well, I think that confirms my suspicion." I thought. I was being monitored by Dr. Ebb's security team. It still didn't concern me much, as nobody was getting in anybody's way. I arrived at the main desk and saw Liz. I walked up to say hi to her. "Hello, how are you, Liz?" She looked up, gave a big smile then just as she was about to say "Hi" back, one of the suit-wearing guys walked up and said to her. "He's not required to sign in. He then turned to me and said, "The Doctor is waiting to see you when you're ready." He then walked a few steps back down the hall to where the examination rooms were. I said to Liz. "Wow, these guys are kind of intimidating." She started talking to me but kept her head down towards the desk and said in mostly a whisper, "Yeah, Hi Matt, it's great to see you. But I've been told not to talk with you." I said, "Really?" She said, "It was strongly recommended, that is all I can say. I don't think you have anything contagious or anything like that or I think they would have mentioned it. But, I think you should go now." With that, I said, "Ok, well, it's great to see you." I kind of wanted to tell her that Cindy and I were on the mend, but at the same time, I also didn't want to tell her. I decided to mention it anyway, "Oh, and by-the-way, Cindy and I are cool again. See you later. Bye." She said, "That's great. I'm happy it worked out. Bye." With that, I moved down the hall to the examination room.

Once inside, another suited guy and Dr. Ebb were waiting. "Ah, Matt, there you are. You're right on time." He motioned for the suit guy to go outside. "Well, how are you doing? Are you feeling all right? Is everything good? Anything different?" Right away I noticed that Dr. J wasn't there. "Where is Dr. J?" I asked. Dr. Ebb answered, "He had another appointment today, and he won't be joining us." That's damn weird I thought. I'm pretty sure I was his prime subject and he wouldn't want to miss any of these sessions, for any reason. As Dr. J readied some equipment I sat there and thought for a moment about telling Dr. Ebb about my self levitation but didn't want for Dr. J to miss any of the "good stuff." "So, anything new?" He asked. I hesitated for a minute but then thought, what the hell. We can fill in Dr. J. later during our next session. I felt like I had to tell someone.

"Dr. Ebb, there is something new that I've figured out." "Oh really? Go on," he said. "Last night, I had the idea that, if I can float all these things, why not try it on myself?" "Interesting." Dr. Ebb was intensely focused on me. "Were you successful?" "Yes, I was," I answered. "Absolutely fascinating", was his response. As I was waiting for him to say something about it, he stepped back and leaned on a table and thought for a minute before continuing.

"Matt, have you told anyone else about this?" "No" I answered. I didn't even think about Cindy knowing. "You are the first, but I was also wanting to let Dr. J know." "I see." He said, "Matt, there is something we must discuss and by all means, I want you to tell me all about this new experience. But first, I'd like to tell you an account of someone." "Sure," I answered. Now, I was the curious one.

Dr. Ebb began, "Have you ever heard of a person by the name of Igor Sikorsky?" "Nope, can't say that I have," I said. Dr. Ebb began, "A long while back, when aviation was just in its infancy, even before flying was a convenient means to travel, there was a young boy who grew up in one of the Russian provinces. This boy was from an average family and had a typical Russian family life. However, this particular boy was startled awake one night to the sound of a loud rhythmic noise. He got up and walked around. While walking, he felt the ground moving and softly vibrating under his feet. In his walking slumber, he looked around. He saw a beautiful room with rows of chairs and opulent surroundings. He went over to the window and looked out. Instead of seeing the cold, snow-covered trees, snow-capped buildings and white roads of a cold Russian winter, he saw palm trees, clear blue/green water, and a beautiful white sandy beach. It was so far removed from anything he'd ever seen before, he didn't know what to think of it.

As this young boy grew up, he eventually immigrated to the United States and became one of the leading pioneers in aviation. For both for the military and in civilian life. He had an extremely successful career as an inventor and became the owner of an aviation company. Even now, he is commonly referred to as, "The father of the helicopter." But this is not quite the end of the story.

In his later years, near the end of his long successful career, he was on board of one of his deluxe aircraft while delivering it to a high-end client in Miami. He said that, during that flight, as he was walking back through the cabin, He, in that instant, knew that this was the same moment he woke to back when he was a boy. It was the same sights, sounds, and feelings he had that one night many, many years ago. He felt the vibration of the aircraft, saw the rows of seats, and then looked out of the window and saw blue water, palm trees, and a white sandy beach."

"Wow!" I told Dr. Ebb. "That's kind of a chilling story." "It is, Matt," said Dr. Ebb, "And here is why I'm telling you this. First, that is a real story, of a real man. But what you don't know is that there are some people, but not many, that have these similar kinds of insights and gifts. In my associations, I've had the responsibility and the pleasure of working with some of these people. In my line of expertise, I've been asked to help find out how these occurrences happen. There have been some people, who I've worked with, and witnessed, that have similar talents as you, however, I've never seen anyone so advanced as you are.

Your levitations are far beyond any that I've come across. You've mentioned thought-reading, and now you say that self flight is within your capability. I think this is just incredible, simply incredible. Your demonstrations are extraordinary. And that brings me to my next thought.

Matt, as you may guess, the brain is an amazingly complicated electrochemical organ. And, there are large gaps in our understanding of it. We are a vastly varied species that houses it. And, we, as a whole, are a constantly changing organism. All life is constantly evolving. Some changes are sometimes beneficial, other times detrimental. The detrimental changes, they usually don't last. Some changes are unnoticeable. And then there are evolutionary leaps. Big changes that occur when conditions are just right, or when there's stress, or, maybe, just by random chance.

From my studies I've noted how man has evolved from ape-like to hunter-gatherers, to agrarian, to the machine age, and now to the current electronic information society. I believe that it's possible, that the next major change is going to be with the human mind. It's taken countless years, but as a species, I think we have finally evolved to the point where bountiful food, shelter, communication, and nearly limitless information is at our fingertips. I often ask myself, what would be next for a developing species?

I have speculated that our next progression would most likely be some form of mental advancement. Maybe an electronic and organic cognizance like an Artificial Intelligence merging with our own. Or possibly, there may be adaptations to the human body by the means of continuously more and more sophisticated implants. Implants blending or integrating with our human bodies until we eventually become something new. However, interestingly enough, and possibly in your case, I think nature may have taken the next step for us. You seem to have bridged what might be the next step in our evolution. You appear to be able to connect to whatever energy that surrounds us and use it to manipulate objects. Maybe it's a connection to the vast amount of "dark matter" or "dark energy" that we can't yet detect in our universe, I'm not sure. But, whatever it is, it needs more study. And, with that said, I'd like to help you.

"Help me how?" I asked.

Besides my personal practice, I'm involved with some government-administered programs. A couple of these specialized departments are where I've been assigned to help, help people like you who exhibit extra abilities. Help people like you, explore their limits. You and the capabilities you possess are the most advanced of anyone I've ever come in contact with, and it's because of your abilities that I'd like for you to come to our facilities where we can test you properly. And frankly, I'd like for this to happen immediately."

Dr. Ebb's request came as a shock and my immediate reaction was pure confusion. I began to rationalize out loud. "But Dr. Ebb, I enjoy my life here. And, I have responsibilities. I don't think I want to go to where ever is it. Where is this place anyway?" Dr. Ebb replied, "I can't say, Matt. But that's only because it's part of the security." "So you're asking me to leave my job, my friends, my girlfriend to go to someplace you can't even tell me where!" "Yes, it's somewhat like that, but it's in the best interest for you and possibly even your country. And, it won't come without some compensation for you. Also, we haven't, after all, excluded the fact that this might be dangerous on some level, or at some time. There's no assurance that there isn't any danger to others for some unseen reason. You wouldn't want to feel responsible for harming something or somebody, even if it was an accident, would you?"

"Hell, now it sounds like you are trying to guilt-trip me into going. I feel like I'm being asked to incarcerate myself." "No, don't think like that at all Matt. We will be continuing our studies on you. Maybe we can find out some of the reasons you can do what you can do. And, also find out if you are in any kind of medical or physical danger. It's not so much a matter about what we don't know right now, but it's more the possibility of what we can find out in the future. Doesn't that sound interesting, even a bit exciting?"

"I don't know. I'll need to do some serious thinking about this Dr. Ebb." "Of course. OK, Matt. I'll give you some time to think. I've got to check in with my office. But please do some serious thinking. I'll be back in short order."

Dr. Ebb left and my mind was reeling. Of course, I want to know what's going on. The "Mr. Fix-it" in me was incredibly curious. But, here is someone wanting to change everything about my life. And he was pressuring me hard to see his way. I felt like I wanted to run away and hide.

CHAPTER 29

The Exodus

Cindy arrived at the hospital early from work and approached the nurse's station. She leaned over the station counter to talk to Liz who was still there working her shift. Hello, I'm Cindy, I'm here to see Matt. "Oh, OH! You're Cindy! Hi, how are you? I remember you. I'm Liz. Oh my! You work here too?" Liz said. "Yes, but I'm over in the children's ward. And, yeah. I remember you too." Said Cindy. Liz remarked, "Matt has talked quite a bit about you." "He has?" Cindy's mind was started to race with female jealousy. "Why is Matt talking about me, to her?" She thought. Liz commented, "Yeah, I'm glad to hear you guys are back on the mend." Cindy replied, "What? Did he say that, did he? And well, yes, since you mentioned it, we're doing fine." Liz answered, "He's a sweet guy. I adore him. But, he's a taken man... he's all wrapped up about you." Cindy's jealously turned over to curiosity and she asked, "So you know a lot about Matt do you?" Liz answered, "Oh, we've talked a bit. He's been quite a regular here lately." At this time one of the suited men walked over to observe. He took a look at the two nurses. Cindy was wearing her nurses uniform, so he assumed that they were workmates and became uninterested and walked off.

Liz lowered her voice and said to Cindy, "They must be doing something pretty important. I've never seen them post a security guard here before let alone two. And I've been instructed not to talk to anybody about who's here or what's been going on." "Oh my, really?" Cindy asked. "Yeah, it's all kind of strange but since I know who you are I think you probably know more than I do." Said Liz."Yeah, Liz, there have been a lot of interesting things going on lately." Cindy commented. "Wow, I sure would like to know." Said Liz. Cindy asked, "Liz, Maybe we can talk later. Where is Matt now?" Liz answered, "He's down the hall, 4th door on the right."

Cindy walked to the door just as Dr. Ebb was leaving the room. He walked out and headed down the hall and passed Cindy in the opposite direction without noticing her. The second suited man was thumbing through his phone while sitting in the hall. He took notice and saw her nurses uniform and hospital badge, and went back to reading his phone. Cindy knocked and walked in.

"Hey, how's it going babe?" She said, "Hey, gorgeous." I answered. "You're early! Everything is fine. But I'll tell you, I'm not liking the way things are going just now. First, Dr. J isn't here and now Dr. Ebb wants me to go to some facility somewhere. He won't tell me where it is or when I'd be coming back, or any other details. I think he wants me to stay there indefinitely. I can't do that. I have a business to run, and of course, there's you."

Cindy said, "Wow, I don't like the sound of that either. I was talking to Liz and she said it's very odd to have security here, and they've asked her not to talk to anybody." "Oh, you've been talking to Liz?" I questioned. I was hoping they weren't having any long discussions, and my mind was started to race about what Liz might have said to Cindy. Me meeting her out, and, the kiss! Oh shit. I may be screwed, I was thinking fast, but Cindy continued. "Yeah, and it seems she knows an awful lot about you." I answered, "She's a nice girl, but too blond for me." I was joking, trying to deflect any interest in Liz. She asked, "So what do they want you to do there? At this facility?" I answered, "I'm not sure, but the doctor says more testing and mentioned helping me find my potential, and to see if what I can do is possibly dangerous, and stuff like that. I think he said they would compensate me.

But I don't have any details. It's the details I need to find out about."

"Well, you'd better find out before you make any decisions.' She said, "I'm going to go and wait for you over by the nurse's station. I'll see you when you're done." Crap, I thought. More time for her to chat with Liz. Maybe that was her intention. I was so ready to get out of there.

Cindy exited the room and headed back down the hall towards the nurse's station. While she was walking back, she saw one of the suited security guys pushing a gurney behind the same doctor that had exited earlier. The doctor was wheeling a small cart towards the examination room. The two men stopped in the hall and the doctor began conversing with the security guard. When she passed them, she could see on the cart there was a vial and a hypodermic syringe. As the doctor noticed her walking by, he stopped talking for a moment and covered the items. He then continued speaking with the security guard. He didn't take much more notice of Cindy in her nurses uniform and hospital badge.

As she was heading back to the nurse's station she kept thinking about the needle on the cart, and the gurney. Her gut feeling was kicking in. She knew that something was wrong. She knew Matt hated needles and that, along with a gurney, had her intuition putting up red flags in her head.

As Cindy reached the nurse's station she was in a mild panic and began to whisper talk with Liz. "Hey Liz, do you know anything about what tests they're doing today with Matt?" Liz answered, "No, they don't tell me anything. Not since Dr. Ebb started working with Dr. J. I used to help Dr. J set up his sessions but... not anymore." Cindy asked, "So, you wouldn't know why or what injections are scheduled, or anything else?" Liz answered, "Nope, is there something wrong?" Liz could tell Cindy was panicking. Cindy told Liz, "Well, I saw that doctor setting up an injection and they have a gurney ready. I know that Matt has a great aversion to needles and injections, and I just know something's not right. I think we need to get him out of there. Is there any way you can help?" Liz thought for a minute and said, "Hummmmm, OK, I think I have an idea. After several moments of hushed discussion, they came up with a plan. Liz said, "OK, I'm going to take my dinner break now.

Are you ready?" Cindy nodded her head and headed down the hall.

Dr. Ebb came back into the examination room and sat down. "Well, Matt. Have you thought about heading to our facilities? We'd love to have you in our care and there's so much we could learn." "Well, Dr. Ebb, I've been thinking about it and I have several questions and..."
Right then there was a knock and the door opened and Cindy entered the room. Dr. Ebb turned around and asked, "Can we help you? You're not supposed to be in here." Cindy
responded, "Oh! Oh yes, I'm so sorry. I'm am sorry to interrupt. But, I've got a message from the front desk for a "Matt" in this room. They said it was urgent." As she was saying her apologies, she discretely moved her hand to her crotch and tapped down between her legs with two fingers while nodding at me. She then handed me a note and turned to exit, again exclaiming, "Here's your message, I'm so sorry to interrupt."

For a brief moment I thought it was a sexual innuendo to me but quickly tossed it aside as I found it curious that she didn't even take a moment to acknowledge that we even knew each other. Or, that she would have given me enough time to introduce her to Dr. Ebb. I opened the note. It was short and cryptic. It said, "Exit out back." Dr. Ebb shook his head in disapproval of the interruption, then turned toward me and started talking again, "So, Matt, everything ok?" Yes," I told him, "Just a work issue that I can take care of later." He said, "Ok good, now then, where were we?" As Dr. Ebb started talking, I was thinking to myself and realized, "She tapped "down there." She wants me to go to the bathroom. Something must be off."

I interrupted Dr. Ebb before he could continue much further. "Umm, Dr. Ebb, I need a minute. Nature calls, I'll be back right back." I went into the bathroom and once in the room turned on a faucet and read the note again.

"Exit out back." I thought for a minute and realized that she wants me to get out of here. Something's not right. My own intuition was telling me the same. All I wanted was to get out of there. Dr. Ebb seemed to be putting undue pressure on me. I needed some time to think. And Cindy's note? That put some urgency in wanting to leave. I stood in there for another minute to gather my wits and to think about how to do this without raising too much suspicion. After a short time, I decided to tell him that it really was an urgent work issue and I really must reschedule. I flushed the toilet and washed my hands for effect. I opened the door and as I exited the bathroom, there was a loud knock at the exam room door and a security guy steps in and loudly pronounced to Dr. Ebb, "She's taken the cart!"

After Cindy had left the room and dropped off the note, she had grabbed the sitting cart in the hall and started wheeling it down the hallway towards the nurse's station. She walked as casually as she could but felt that she was trembling so hard that everyone could see. However, to everyone else, she looked so inconspicuous that the security guard didn't realize anything was amiss. She made it to the nurse's station, passed the other guard, and started trotting ever faster to the front exit. About this time the security guard by the examination room looked up from his phone and noticed the missing cart. He got up and banged on the exam room door and then stepped through. He then loudly pronounced, "She's taken the cart!" Dr. Ebb and the guard then both went running down the hall towards the entrance.

I watched Dr. Ebb leave the room. I then looked out into the hall I saw both Dr. Ebb and the security guys running towards the front exit. That's' when I went the opposite direction. I quickly made my way to the security doors at the far end of the building. I hesitated for a second as the sign on the doors said, "Alarm will sound."

Dr. Ebb and the security guys bolted out of the hospital entrance only to find a utility cart sitting outside by the traffic circle, minus the syringe and vial. As they were scanning the parking lot, they saw Cindy's car peeling out through the lot and out onto the road. The two security guards rushed to one of the parked government SUV's and took off after her. They made chase and quickly began to close the distance. They followed for several blocks and got to within a few hundred yards from her vehicle. The car then made an abrupt turn into a fast-food parking lot and screeched into an empty parking spot. They raced in and immediately boxed in the car. The two guards got out of their SUV and began to approach the car on both sides from behind. As they got close, they saw a blond-haired girl looking into the side view mirror putting on hot pink lipstick. As they looked in, they heard Liz exclaim with a girlish laugh, "So, don't you guys just love this place? Like, everybody does!"

At the hospital, I went ahead and pushed open the doors and walked outside to the back parking lot. I went outside and stood there for a minute not sure of what to do next. For several moments, with the alarms echoing through the air, I thought about what to do next. It was then that I saw an odd car racing through the lot only to pull up right next to where I was standing. As it stopped, I heard Cindy's voice say, "Hurry up, get in!" I looked in to see her driving the car! I went around and jumped into the front seat. Cindy started driving off almost before the door closed. As I buckled in I asked, "Who's car is this. What's going on?" Cindy continued to drive out of the parking lot and away from the hospital. Then she said, "Look at this!"

She handed me a cloth napkin which I unrolled to see a syringe and a small vial. "What's this?" I ask. She said, "THAT, was for you." "What do you mean?" I asked her. She told me, "They had this there for you, and, there was a gurney prepped and ready to go. I didn't like the look of things so I felt like I had to do something to get you out of there." "Holy shit," I exclaimed. " You might be right. I think they intended to take me to some facility, whether I decided to go or not. Where are we going? And, where did you get this car?" I asked. Cindy answered, "This is Liz's car. She said she'd help." "Liz's car?" I asked. Cindy said, "Yeah, we thought that they probably know what mine and your cars look like since we saw them parking outside your place. So, she let me borrow her car." "Ok, Wow! Cool. That's pretty smart," I commented. "And, damn nice of her."

"What's this about them taking you somewhere?" Cindy asked. "Well, Dr. Ebb was trying to convince me to go to some facility somewhere." Was my answer. "Oh my! I knew something was up!" She was proud of her intuition but also mad at Dr. Ebb at the same time. "Where should we go? I don't know what to do next." She asked. I told her, "I think we need some time to think. I also think we can't go home as that might be one of the first places they'd look. I'm going to call Mike and see if he can meet us somewhere."

I called Mike and told him we would meet him at Keegan's bar in a couple of hours. A few hours later, we pulled up and went inside. As we approached the booth where Mike and Phyllis sitting, I could see another man sitting with them. I was a little hesitant to approach because I'd never seen this person before, but I still wanted to talk with Mike. I needed his input to help me think things through. He had always been a good sounding board when I had problems. I believe it was because when I'd vocalize troubles to him, I could hear the issues out loud. Then, they'd be easier for me to analyze.

As we came up to the table my fear was somewhat reduced as I could see the white-collar of the clergy. Phyllis introduced us, "Hi Cindy, Hi Matt, I'd like you to meet my friend, priest William Bishop. He's the son of Father Raymond Bishop, that famous exorcist that worked on a real case in St. Louis a long while back. The one they wrote the book about and made the movie "The Exorcist." We were just talking with him when you called Mike."

I was flabbergasted, "You've got to be kidding. You want me to talk to a priest? So you're thinking I need to be exorcised?" Phyllis explained, "Well, Matt, you've got to agree, there is something unnatural about you and I think you might need this kind of help." The father started to chime in, "You know Matt, that there are things in this world that are..." I interrupted his instant sermon. "I don't need exercising, what I do need is some help from my friends. Mike, can I talk to you in private?"

Mike and I excused ourselves to go sit in another booth. "Mike, what the hell dude? Why did you let her bring this religious crap here? Mike, shrugged and said, "Well, we were going to call you this evening to ask to come by, but you called us first. Phyllis and I were thinking, that since we all hang out together all the time, and, since you've asked us for some help, this is what Phyllis came up with to help you with your problem. You know she just wants to help. I was thinking that she might be more accepting of you, of all this, if you just talked with the father a little bit. I mean she may have a point, I don't know. I just want her to feel secure. I'm sorry if this is bad timing or something."

I told Mike, "Bad timing might just be exactly what this is. You should know I don't need any other people finding out whats going on, because, I may not even know what's going on. Let me tell you what happened just a while ago. Cindy and I just "escaped" from the hospital where I've been doing the testing." "Escaped?" He asked. I said, "Yeah. A doctor there is associated with some government programs and was probably going to ship me to some facility to who-knows-where. Now we need to figure out what to do." "Wow, that's serious," Mike said while shaking his head in disbelief. "What do you want to do?" He asked. I told him, "I don't know. I need some time to think. I mean, what does someone do when you think the government wants to keep you."

Mike said, "Shit man. I don't know. That's some heavy stuff. But, I think I may have an idea for you. If you need a place to think, that is. I know a place you can go to." "Really? What? Where?" I asked. I wanted to know. "My family has a hunting shack in the hills. We've had it forever. It was my great granddad's place a long time ago. It was passed to my dad and it'll be passed to me after him. We could go there. It's not around anything and it's fully stocked with everything for hunting season. It's not hunting season yet, so, no one will be there."

"Wow Mike, that sounds pretty good." I was excited about the idea. Mike then said, "Ok, great. I already feel like I own it, but, just to let you know, it's pretty far away from everything. There's not any electricity, phone service, or even running water." "That's fine Mike. It sounds perfect. But wait a minute. You've got to be shitting me. So, for as long as I've known you, why didn't you tell me about this place before? We could have hung out there for some fun." I was a little miffed that he had kept this place a secret. "I didn't think you liked hunting." He answered. "Damn Mike," I explained, "You don't have to hunt to hang out in the woods. We could go hiking, make campfires, wildlife watch, whatever, just enjoy nature. But, that's "ok." I do think that's a great idea. Let's get rid of the father and then figure out how to get to your shack. Do you mind if we crash at your place tonight?" "Sure. No problem." He said. At that moment, I was thinking to myself how great it was to have a good friend.

We went back to the booth and made plans for Phyllis to take the priest back to his car. I thanked her for her concern and made an apology to them both for being so abrupt and short with them earlier. "It had been a stressful day," I told them. We didn't tell them any details on what had happened earlier in the day, or what we talked about, or what we'd planned on for later. We all left the pub and Cindy, Mike and I crashed at Mike's place that evening. I barely slept at all, but not sleeping gave me time to think about what we were going to do next.

CHAPTER 30

The Wooded Timeout

In the morning Cindy called her office and told them that she had a family emergency and needed a few days off. I called my foreman and told him the same. We then drove two cars, Mike's and Liz's, to the hospital. When we pulled up we looked for but didn't see any government type vehicles in the parking lot. We found Cindy's car where Liz had parked it, and mine was right where I had left it. We didn't want to approach them should the government guys be lurking around. Once we figured it was all clear, we parked Liz's car and let Mike take Liz's keys to her. We also gave Mike a note explaining to her that we were heading out of town for a few days and thanked her for her amazing help. We told him to be on the lookout for any suited guys with military-type hair cuts. Mike successfully delivered the keys and the note and then we set off to the hunting shack. He said he didn't see any suited guys in the hospital but confessed, he probably wouldn't know what to look for even if he did see anyone.

Mike, Cindy and I were just exiting the city when I got a phone call on my cell phone. It was a number I didn't recognize. The number was showing, but it didn't have an identifying name of who it was. I picked up the call only to find out it was none other than Dr. Ebb. "Matt, this is Dr. Ebb. I'd like to talk with you. We realize that you may have some reservations about coming to work with us. You must understand that we need to find out the particulars about you and your case. There are concerns that we have to consider and only by having you with us, in a safe environment, can we evaluate what the implications are. You must see that. It can be a matter of public safety as well as protection for you and possibly a learning experience for all. Can I meet with you somewhere to discuss your options?"

"I don't think that it's such a good idea, Dr. Ebb. From my angle, I noticed that, for one, Dr. J. is no longer in the loop with us, and, that bothers me. He's a good doctor and I have come to trust him and now that he's not with us, I'm concerned. And two, I found out there was an injection, and a gurney, waiting for me at our last meeting. That's a REALLY big problem for me. Along with your recent monitoring of my activities, like at my home and the hospital. This doesn't give me much confidence in your intentions. I think I'm going to take a few days off, think about things, and when I'm ready, I'll contact you. So for now, good-bye."
Just before I hung up Dr. Ebb told me, "Ok Matt, but if you want to get in contact with me, please use this number."

I hung up the call and turned to Cindy and Mike, "Hey guys, that was Dr. Ebb. He was trying to get me to come and meet with him. I don't remember ever giving him my phone number but he probably got it from the hospital records. Anyway, I'm pretty sure that, if they have our numbers, I would guess that they can probably track our phones. I think it would be a good idea if we turn our phones off for a while. I don't think they'll be able to find us with our phones turned off. Mike, you can turn yours back on after you've gotten back to town, but not before. And I mean off-off, as in powered down." Everybody agreed and shut off their phones.

Mike, Cindy, and I drove for a few hours until we reached the hunting shack. It was a small simple place but exactly what one would want to get away from everything. An idyllic log wood cabin with a rustic fireplace, cords of wood lining the outside walls, and inside there were a couple of single beds. Cans of food and dried meats were hanging, with sundries on the shelves, an ammo loading press, a hand pump sink, and various stuffed animal heads and skins on the walls. There was no electricity and most likely no cell signals. We let Mike turn his phone on for just a few minutes to verify and we verified there were no signal bars, connections, or anything. Nice and remote. This was a beautiful place and we felt secure that it was far from everybody and everything. It really was the perfect place to get away from it all. Mike said his goodbyes and made plans to come back to check on us in a couple of days.

Cindy and I sat down at the center table and looked at each other. "Well, Mike's gone." "Yep." "So what do we do now?" she asked. I answered, "I have a few ideas. But, first, since we ARE all alone, with no one to interrupt, and nothing to do at this particular moment. I think you should come over here, sit on my lap, and we'll find something interesting to do. She obliged.

The excitement of the previous day had heightened our senses. We were alive with the rush of having done something totally unexpected, maybe even a little dangerous. Without realizing it, we found ourselves "on-the-run." It was the thrill of the chase. It's said by behaviorists that people get aroused when exposed to violence or aggression. It's an ingrained reaction. This must have been the same mechanism that was working on us.

We kissed and rubbed our hands on each other until buttons were found and undone. Zippers were slowly unzipped and skin that was being revealed got the attention of lip peppered kisses and hand explored touches. As new areas got their care, a moment's return to passionate kissing brought back to focus the person we were enjoying. Then, as the body voyage continued, on to the next area that needed exploring.

Area by area, space by space, shoulders to stomach, to thighs. Pants were pulled off and legs were uncovered. The caressing and undressing continued, all unhurried, with the knowledge that we had no place to be and no schedule to keep. At last, with our body temperatures raised by the anticipation, and with our bodies fully uncovered and our souls ready to connect, we laid down together and tasted and touched and kissed each other as our coupled heat combined and enveloped us. We made love and even after our first peak together, we continued kissing, kissing through the release. We were awash in passionate energy. We continued, as though we were on a cliff overlooking a vista and struck dumb by its beautiful intensity. Intensity so alluring that it dared us to get ever closer and closer to the edge. Then the edge came, again. Our free fall expressed itself in simultaneous exhaled screams like the spontaneous yell of a base jumper when taking that weightless step into the abyss. With the exhilaration and free-fall finished, we slept the remainder of the afternoon, naked and satisfied.

We woke up in the early evening and rummaged up a scrumptious dinner consisting of bacon and beans. I was amused by the fact that it was cooked in a black round kettle over a wood-burning fireplace. "This is so rustic," I told her. "And, this dinner may be a bit interesting. Beans and bacon might make for a noisy night!"

We both laughed and I told her how exquisite the afternoon had been. I remarked how brave and smart she was to get us out of the hospital. Then she asked, "Matt, how long do you think you want to stay here? We can't stay here forever. It's not a bad place to hang out for a while but, at some point, we'll have to go." I said, "You're right, but for the time being, at least until Mike comes back, let's just enjoy this place, and us being together. I feel like this is a little vacation, and, it's not costing us anything. I couldn't have planned a better getaway."

We sat in front of the fire wrapped in a blanket and enjoyed the rest of the evening watching the embers burn down until they lost their orange glow. I found myself watching an ember that would turn gray, then flake off only to reveal a new orange ember underneath until those too, turned gray, then gone. We both fell asleep drifting off to the smoky aromas and rich wood quietness of the cabin, feeling both warm and loved.

CHAPTER 31

Base Camp

The next couple of days we enjoyed the woods around the cabin. There was something completely rejuvenating about not having an agenda and nobody around. There were no schedules to keep, no grumpy clients, workers, patients, or co-workers to deal with and nothing but the quiet and the sounds of the woods. We took long hikes and splashed in the stream. We'd take showers in the rainwater catch that ran off the roof, and it was so cold! Dinners were an adventure as we'd have to make whatever we could using only the supplies in the cabin. In the evenings after we ate we'd sit in front of the fire and have small talk. I decided not to do any of my lifting or levitating. I knew that was the reason that we were hiding out and I thought it was better for us to have this fabulous downtime. Making love was often and intense. It's amazing how much better ones' body works when the stresses of everyday life are taken away.

One evening, after a particularly satisfying lovemaking encounter, Cindy brought us back the reality of our situation. "Matt, Mike is coming back in the morning. I assume we're going to go back with him?" I said, "Yeah, I think I'm going to track down Dr. J when we get back. I want to talk with him and see what he says. I also want to see if those government guys are still stalking us at my house. I'll also call Dr. Ebb with a borrowed phone or a payphone or something, and ask him what he thinks my options are at this point. I'll also ask him what his real intentions are. It can't hurt. I mean, are we sure that going to that "place" is the only option? Maybe, after all, the best option IS to go to that "place." I don't know what to think. Also, once we're back, I think I'll look up what it takes to lose your identity and start a new life. If it should ever have to come to that. I mean, what does someone do when you think the government wants you? I'm only trying to get some ideas." "Gawd, you think we'll have to do all that?" She replied, definitely worried. I tried to re-assure her, "I certainly hope not, but it might be necessary. Let's hope it won't come to that."

The next morning Cindy and I got up. We laughed at each other as we took some very fast, very cold showers again in the rain-catch shower. We then cooked breakfast and tidied up the cabin. We sat in the wood rockers on the front porch and waited for Mike to arrive. Before long we heard a car coming up the forest road. It was Mike. He pulled up and greeted us, "So how's it going, guys? Did you survive?" "Mike, thanks so much for letting us stay here. It was great to get away from it all. Cindy and I really enjoyed your place. We cleaned up pretty well inside. Do we owe you anything, for anything? For food, gas?" Mike said, "No, we're good." It hadn't been but a few minutes after Mike arrived when he stopped talking for a second, then asked, "Can you guys hear that?"

Right then, we heard a faint thumping noise coming from down in the valley. "What's that? The noise grew a little louder and seemed so out-of-place from the peace and quietness we'd had since we'd been there. After a few short few moments of strain-ing to hear, it quickly became so loud we could feel it in our chests. Then we saw it. A helicopter made a pass directly over-head then started making a large circle around the cabin.

"Holy shit!" I said, "I think they found us. I think they followed you. Mike, where's your phone?" Mike got out his phone and looked at it. "Aww crap! I left my phone on." He lamented. "But, I didn't think anyone could track out here anyway, there's no sig-nal." I said, "Well, I imagine they tracked you as far as they could and got an idea of the direction you were heading. But, what's done is done."

Mike said, "I'm pretty sure there's no place for them to land around here. They might have an idea where we are, but they're going to have to drive to get here. "Ok, that gives us some time." I thought about our options for a moment, then said, "Mike, if it's all right with you I'd like to borrow some stuff out of the cabin." "Sure," he answered. "Cindy lets grab some supplies, we'll try to lose them in the forest."

We got a couple of backpacks and loaded them up with some essentials including a map and a GPS that was always on a constant charge from a solar panel on the roof of the cabin. Mike said they used it to keep track of hunting spots and it saved them time when returning after a hunt. I told him we were borrowing them but will give them back when we meet back in the city.

I instructed Mike, "Mike, we're going to hike awhile to get them off our trail. In a couple of days, we'll contact you and go from there." I gave Mike my laptop that I had brought with us when we had left the city. I had wanted to write down some notes and ideas as well as make a game plan for when we eventually returned. As Cindy stuffed our backpacks with supplies, I talked with Mike a few minutes more before he headed back. We saw and heard the helicopter make a couple of passes over the trees and it was a good bet that they were looking for a place to land. Mike had suggested that it was far too hilly and had too many trees for them to find a landing area close by and I was pretty sure he was right. If they want to get here, they were going to have to come by road.

We said our goodbye's and Mike took off back down the access road. I asked him to leave his phone on, but to drive to another town in the opposite direction. Maybe they would take the bait and follow him thinking that he had picked us up. I got out the borrowed map and searched for an area that looked remote but wasn't too far from a town where we could hop on a bus or get a taxi. Then, Cindy and I started our trek through the woods.

Cindy asked, "I hope you know where you're going. I don't like the idea of being in the woods for an extended time, especially if we get lost. And, I have to get back to work sometime. I don't know how I'm going to explain it to them when I get back. I hope they let me keep my job. The only good thing for me is there is a need for nurses everywhere. I thought the cabin was nice, but the forest is dirty and uncomfortable and I'm dying to have a hot shower sometime soon." I said to her, that, "I have to get back to my clients too," and reassured her, "It was only for a day, or maybe two." And to, "Enjoy the experience." She didn't protest anymore out loud, but, she didn't look happy about it either. We kept on hiking.

After nearly half-day of making our way through the woods, we arrived at an area that had looked good on the map. Fortunately, it was indeed a good spot. It had water from a clear running stream, and I found a nice open level area for the small popup tent we had. As twilight fell, the night was clear and bright. We made a dinner of a couple of military MRE's (Military, Meal-Ready-to-Eat) and afterward, sat together to look at the stars. It must have been a meteor shower that evening for, as soon as we'd see one streak of light, another would shortly follow. With us being so far from concentrated light, and in a small opening away from the canopy of trees, the clear night air was giving us a really good show. After a short while of snuggling together and counting meteors, we realized that all the hiking during the day had tired us out. We decided we'd sit for a little while longer and watch the sky before going to bed.

After we saw one especially large meteor that broke into pieces before burning out, Cindy brought up what was bothering her, "Matt, what are we going to do? Can we go back to our normal lives after all this? Will they take you away? I don't want things to change. I thought we were going to have a real-life together. Tell me everything is going to be Ok? It will be, won't it?" I re-assured Cindy. "Yeah, babe. Everything is going to be all right. I'm sure you don't need to worry about anything. Once we re-turn to the city, I'll have those talks with Dr. J and Dr. Ebb. After that, I'm sure we can go back to the way things were." To me, I felt like I was lying. I wasn't sure at all what was going to happen. But, I think Cindy needed to hear that everything was going to be "all right." I knew the "worry" that women always carry was bubbling up and I wanted to make it as stress-free for her as possible. I commented, right after another big meteor passed, "There's a good one, make a wish and we'll go to bed." She did, and after that, we went inside the tent to sleep. Our sleeping bags felt warm, dry, and comfortable. We were asleep in minutes.

The next morning we woke at daybreak and we took a quick towel bath in the clear stream water. We made and drank some instant coffee and then packed up our gear. While looking at the map I said, "I think we can make this town in a few hours and then we'll be able to get a bus or taxi back to the city. We might even spend another night before going back if you're not in a hurry. But if we do, I'll get a motel so you can get that hot shower you've been dreaming about." "Oh my, that would be great." She said. "I'd rather be at home but a hot shower anywhere would be fabulous!"

I checked the map and GPS and decided on what appeared to be the most direct route to town and we took off in that direc-tion. I thought it rather fortunate that we hadn't seen or heard any helicopters since we left the hunting cabin. I assumed that whoever came to look for us had probably made it to the cabin and then given up once it was discovered no one was there. Or, maybe they took the bait and went after Mike. "Oh shit!" I thought out loud to myself, "I hope I haven't caused some prob-lems for Mike. I can't imagine he could be in trouble for anything."

Up till now, I reasoned, this plan seemed to be working. Once back, we'd have the time to contact people at our discretion and not on someone else's agenda. I believed that they were just interested in what I can do for them and that we hadn't broken any laws that I knew of. So, we shouldn't be in any real trouble.

After hiking for about an hour or so, we noticed a small plane flying above the trees. It wouldn't normally be of any attention, seeing a plane fly by, but this one seemed to be flying in a pattern that was extra low and slow, and it came back by regularly. After about the 4th pass it was definite that it was us they were looking for. I told Cindy, "I think they might be using infrared to look for us. Because, they seem to be sweeping by and around us a lot, and pretty low. Otherwise, I don't think they can see us through all these trees. I think the only way we're going to be able to lose them is to get to town and blend in with the locals. Then we can find our ride to the city and get in touch with Mike. Let's pick up the pace."

We quickened our trek through the woods trying to maintain a path that stayed under the canopy of tree cover. We eventually arrived at a dirt road that crossed our way and since it generally went in direction of town, I thought it would give Cindy a much-needed break to travel on a shady, tree-lined, level road for awhile. It was far easier than navigating around rocks and dodging bushes. We walked on the dirt road until we came upon some big boulders where I decided we needed a break from the rapid walk we were having. "Here's good Cindy. Let's take a break for a few minutes." Cindy and I sat down and took off our packs. We got out some water and Cindy asked me, "How much farther do you think it is?" She had been silent for the entire morning and I was thinking about how good a sport she was being with all this hiking.

Before I could answer her, we heard a vehicle coming up the

road. "Quick, grab the packs!" We grabbed our gear and hid behind the boulders. I thought we were way to close to the road and it made me nervous. As we watched, we saw two black SUV's pass by. They were driving slow and I recognized them as the same two SUV's we'd seen days prior at the hospital. As they continued down the road they eventually disappeared behind a curve. I told Cindy, "Let's get off this road and get some space from those SUV's. Did you see that they were the same cars we saw the other day?" She agreed and we grabbed our packs and made a sprint into the woods. We jogged at a quick pace and when we felt we were a good distance from our encounter we slowed and walked at a more casual pace.

Cindy decided to speak up, "Ok Matt, they're definitely wanting to pick you up. I'm so worried. How long do you think we can evade them? They're going through a hell of an effort to get to you." "I know what you mean." I sympathized. "I've got to contact Mike, Dr. J, and possibly the police. But for now, we'll try to stick to the plan." "Wait for a second! Be quiet!" Cindy said as she stopped in her tracks. "Stand still, listen... I hear dogs." There was barking and howling coming from behind us, and getting louder. "Drop the packs," I said. "We've got to get out of here. Let's go!" We left the packs near the edge of a large pasture and started running. Across the far end of the pasture was a farmhouse. "Look there's a farm. We must be getting near the edge of town. Head that way." I said. As we ran we could hear the dogs barking behind us. They were on our trail and although we were running at a good clip the dogs seemed to be keeping pace with us. For some short moments, the dogs would stop their barking and it seemed as though they'd lose our trail. Then, and it wouldn't take long, and they'd get the scent back, and the howling would become loud and fast again. We were ahead for now, but the problem was, we were getting tired.

Just as we approached the farm I looked back across the field and I saw the dogs exiting the woods on the far side. Again, they would stop, sniff out an area, catch the scent and start howling and running. I knew if we stopped running, it wouldn't take them long to reach us. We banged on the farmhouse door. No answer. The door was locked and no one could be seen inside. We dashed to the barn. I hoped that we could get in there and find something to use to fight off the dogs. Or better yet, a car, tractor, 4 wheeler, anything. We frantically searched. There was nothing. We couldn't find a way into the barn and there were no tools to be used as weapons. We could now hear that the dogs were almost near the house.

We were just about to run again, but I halted for a second, then shouted to Cindy, "Stop!.... Wait. Hold on for a minute." She stopped but said frightfully, "We got to go!" I could tell she wanted to keep running. "No, wait. It's Ok." I stood still. I closed my eyes. I breathed in deep and slowed my breath, then relaxed my body. I told my heart to beat slower, slower, slow. I emptied and calmed my mind. Then I concentrated and focused. I waited.

One after the other the dogs rounded the corner of the barn at a quick gallop. I held my hand out in an effort to stretch my senses. I sensed the movement of the dogs. I could almost feel them. I felt their hearts pounding. I imagined that I could see them lifting off the ground. Even though my eye's where shut, I could see them, imagine them. Four dogs in a single line, one after the other rounding the corner of the barn. I then heard Cindy say, "Oh my god."

I squinted my eyes open and saw them. The dogs began lifting off the ground. Their legs were pumping midair, full speed, as their bodies rose. They began twisting their heads back and forth in every direction in a panic. Their barking turned to loud yelping and fearful yaps. They were terrified.

The dogs had stopped and were now about two to three feet off the ground. I stayed collected and relaxed with my eyes barely open. Not losing my concentration, I decided I wanted to see what the dogs looked like with the glasses on as they floated. It was the first time I had floated an animal. I calmly reached in my pocket and pulled out a pair of the magician's glasses and put them on. I further opened my eyes and saw a purple fog surrounding each dog. A misty halo around every one of them with a thin wisp of purple ether stretching between them. Like a string of dog pearls floating a few feet above the ground.

I let my concentration diminish. The fog vanished and the dogs dropped to the ground. Not hurt, but scared, they immediately reversed their direction and started running off, full speed, back towards the direction of where they came. Much faster than they how they had chased us, with a continuous yipping and yelping loudly as they left. I let out a deep breath and said to Cindy, "How about that?" I was feeling proud. "Wow, just wow." She commented. I think she was at a loss for any other words. I said, "I think the people running those dogs must not be far behind. Let's go. I'm sure the town is getting pretty close." We left the farm and continued towards town.

CHAPTER 32

My Flight

We walked from farm to farm along the road towards town. Although we knew that it was a bigger risk being on the road, from our recent experience, it was better to make fast travel and walk roadside rather than cross rough country. We kept an ear and eye out for vehicles and whenever we thought we heard a car coming we'd dash into the woods or hide wherever possible. Fortunately, we didn't see any cars in a couple of miles. We were making good time. I could see that we must have been on the outskirts of town and it was confirmed by a small subdivision of houses. And, we could see taller "in town" buildings some distance past them. Cindy hadn't said a word since we left the farmhouse. I couldn't decide if it was because she was tired, or simply bewildered about the floating dogs. Maybe she was ignoring the fact that we were being pursued. Maybe she was trying to piece it all together. Maybe she had had enough. I kept my thoughts to myself as we walked.

We entered the subdivision from what must have been a back entrance. We walked along the main drive until we had gotten about halfway through. Then, at the subdivision front entrance, we saw a black SUV turn in. "Over here!" I shouted. I grabbed Cindy and immediately we ran between a couple of the closest houses and found a corner that had large tall bushes to conceal ourselves, yet we could still see the road. My first thought was, I hope they hadn't seen us, and my professional second thought was, that these bushes were way overgrown and in severe need

of pruning. However, at that moment, I was glad that they pro-
viding a good place to hide. Our hearts raced as a single black
SUV drove by. We watched and was relieved to see it go past us
and continue. It went down to the far end of the street and made
a turn. They hadn't seen us.

As we stood there enveloped in the large bush, Cindy broke her
silence. "Matt, what are we doing?" I could tell she was tired. I
thought to myself, I have a very strenuous job and I was used to
walking and being physical for hours and hours every day. This
was not as taxing for me as it was for her. And, I knew that if I
was feeling fatigued. She must be, for sure, be worn out. Being
away from home, the camping, the hikes, the walking and the
running, it had all taken its toll. She was exhausted.

I knew I had to change plans. I thought for a moment and decided that the right thing to do was to let Cindy go on alone.
"Cindy, I want you to head back without me. I know it's me
they're chasing. I think you should find a way back. I'll find my
way to you later, but for now, I think it's a good idea if you head
out. You can go into town and get a taxi, or bus, or call Mike, or
have someone give you a ride. Maybe get a hotel room for a night
and get that hot shower you've been dreaming of. I think it's best
if I head back and find the camping gear we dropped and stay
away for another day or two. When I can, I'll call you or Mike and
let you know when I can make it back. So, don't worry and wait
for my call." Cindy said a little relieved, "Are you sure? I want
to know you'll be alright, but, I'm so tired." I told her, "Yes, I'll
be fine. Besides, you know how I like camping." Cindy said, "Ok.
I think I'll go get a room first. That shower sounds like the best
thing ever." I answered, "Then that's it." I decided I'd at least get
her checked in to a hotel or motel so I told her, "We'll both go to
a hotel and get you checked in." At that moment I thought that I
might be able to join her.

Just as we were about to leave the bushes, the black SUV came
out of a closer side street. We ducked back behind the bushes

again and waited for it to pass. After it went by, Cindy looked at me and said, "I think I should go into town alone. I assume they figured we were heading to this town and now they're patrolling the streets. I don't want you to get caught." I stood and thought again for a minute. I didn't like the idea of Cindy being alone and on her own in a strange town but I couldn't see any alternative. She couldn't keep going and I needed to keep evading the security guys. I told her, "I hate to leave you by yourself, you sure you're going to be alright?" She said, "Yeah, I'll be fine. I'm a big girl." What she said made me not want to let her go on alone, even more. I told her, "Ok then, big girl. But be extra careful. You know I love you? Like, crazy love? Crazy big love?" "No, you're not crazy," she said, "But you are weird."

We laughed and hugged and then made sure she had her phone, some bank cards, and some cash. "I'll see you in a few days. Use the cash first. And, don't turn on your phone until you have to. I'll contact you, or Mike, later. And stay out of sight of those SUV's!" She said, "Ok, see you later, love you!" After a long kiss, she started walking towards town.

I started back in the direction of the farmhouse. I figured it would take time to get back and try to locate the packs. Hopefully, I'd still have enough daylight to find myself a good spot to camp. As I walked, I couldn't help but worry about Cindy. I was already regretting my decision. A strange girl in a strange town. What if she got into trouble? What could she do? Who would know she was there? I was feeling despicable. I had to put it out of my mind.

After a shorter time than I thought, I made it back to where we had our run to the farmhouse. Once there, it was a short walk back to where we dropped the packs. I realized that the first time you go somewhere it seems to take longer than subsequent repeat visits. Maybe it's the mind trying to store data points of new surroundings. For instance, when you go to the neighborhood supermarket. The first time you go, it seems far. You may remember the full 20 minutes it took to get there. But, after months or even years of repeated trips, you forget the distance entirely. You hop in the car, switch on the radio, and before you realize it, you're there. This was my trek back. Seemingly difficult to get to where I wanted to go, easy to get back to where I was.

I was fortunate that the person or persons that were running the dogs hadn't found the packs. I guessed that the dogs might have run by and sniffed them on their way to us. Nonetheless, I was glad to find them. I consolidated most of the items from both packs into one and checked my map to figure out a suitable location for my next camp. I decided to make my way to the town down the valley thinking that the rough terrain would make it more difficult should anyone fly over and try to locate me. I hiked for a couple of hours and just before dark, I found, next to a cliff face, a nice dry little hollow, kind of a short cave, that was out of sight of flying things and out of the wind and weather. It was a good spot to wait out the night before heading on.

I stayed overnight in the shelter of the cave. In the morning I wasn't as rested as I hoped to be. I hadn't slept at all. I worried about Cindy the entire night. And, I started worrying about myself. I thought about the effort that Dr. Ebb, or more likely what the "government" was spending on me. Planes, Helicopters, chase dogs... It seemed that I didn't have much of a chance. Maybe I should submit, become the lab rat. The best-case scenario? Be employed by some government agency like an indentured servant. I fought off the negative thoughts and decided to keep trying to make my way to the next town, then hopefully, back to the city.

I got an early start. After all, I had hardly slept at all. The cave was uncomfortable and all I wanted to do was to get back to Cindy, talk to Dr. J. and try to get my life in order. So off I went in the direction of town number two. I made my path making sure I kept a respectable distance to any roads and kept an ear out for anything out of the ordinary. It seemed to turn out that it was further away than I estimated. Probably because of the rough terrain, it was probably going to take me another day, maybe more, to make it to that town. And, during my hike, if I thought a plane was to fly over, I would bury myself in some vegetation or hide under my pack and hunker down close to a tree. Fortunately, it didn't appear that anyone was on my trail and no planes flew over. Maybe, if lucky, I had shaken them. But still, in the back of my mind, I was super worried about Cindy, and even a bit concerned about Mike. I felt like I had turned them both into the bait.

My hiking went well and according to my map, I was getting close to town #2. I thought it'd be better if I stayed just outside of town instead of going in and renting a motel room, even though the thought of a warm dry room and a soft bed was starting to seem like a very attractive idea. I thought it easier to not get caught in town and better to wait till morning so it would be easier to get a bus or some ride back to the city. On the map, I found a state park just outside of town and thought, "What a great place to camp. I could get a hot shower, a level campsite and I'd blend in with the other campers." So that's what I did. I walked to the park, through the entrance gate and paid a $10 entrance and campsite fee. I then found my campsite and set up camp.

This night's sleep was going to be much better than the nights before. I took a nice hot shower in the community bathhouse and was just about to make myself another MRE for dinner when some nearby campers walked by and started a conversation. I learned they were from out-of-state and were trying to work their way around to visit all the continental 49 states and even Alaska. I was impressed that they had already visited 31. And their camper wasn't any bigger than a 2-bed popup. I figured they must have indeed been to 31 of the states, as it had the "state" stickers to prove it!

That evening, along with a few other campers and some of their kids, I ended up sitting around their glowing campfire till late in the evening. We had hamburgers, swapped stories, made S'more's, and sang songs. It was fun. It's the kind of entertainment that camping can be. Go places, meet people, have fun hearing stories, and sharing food. For that, I embrace the camper's life. It's easy joy and exploration. The meeting of new people and seeing new places. But mainly, it's leaving the stresses of work and home behind. It was a good distraction for me. The company of warm-hearted strangers helped keep my mind off of Cindy and of being pursued. Nonetheless, way before the time that I was ready to crawl into my sleeping bag, I was wishing Cindy had come with me. I was thinking she would have loved this. I was missing my sleeping partner again.

In the morning I woke refreshed and with a much better focus on what I wanted to do. I made myself a small "MRE" breakfast and topped it off with yet another instant coffee. Then packed up camp and headed towards town. I was determined to get some sort of transit back to the city. There, I could make calls, see Cindy, recover my car, and get in touch with Mike and Dr. J. Hopefully, somehow, get back to life as usual.

I hiked away from the park and after a short time checked the map to see my progress. I was following a highway down to the valley towards town. The town must have been getting close as houses were getting and more numerous and I could see the buildings down in the valley. Upon reaching the levelness of the valley there was a roadside diner. I decided it would be great to have a hot lunch and a rest before heading into town. I sat down and ordered a plate of fried corn beef hash, a BLT sandwich, and a couple of medium fried eggs and a chocolate milkshake. It was a far cry better than a cold MRE. The past few days hiking had made me insatiably hungry! I was so happy to take a load off my feet and to have someone else prepare me a meal. It felt good that I had time to relax for a minute, and was hopeful that my trip back to the city was going to be an easy one.

I was halfway through my lunch when a black SUV pulled into the parking lot. It was the government security guys. As they parked their car I couldn't decide what to do. Run, hide? I knew I couldn't make it out the front door in time without them noticing. I decided to sit at the bar, and try to blend in and hopefully not get spotted. Kind of like hiding in plain sight. I was nervous as the two military crew-cut men came in and found a booth along the front wall. They didn't seem to be looking for anything except a hot lunch and I tried to remain inconspicuous as possible and made a conscious effort not to look their way. Then, as casually and quietly as I could, I asked the waitress for the check and paid my bill. I could hear them order coffee and discuss the menu as I left. It must have been when they saw me put on my pack outside that they noticed me. As I walked past the front of the diner, I could see through the window, the two men get up from their booth. I thought, "Damn, they've seen me!" I started running in the direction of town.

As I glanced back, I could see them exiting the diner and running to their SUV. My only thought was to get into town and find a taxi, get a bus, hitch a ride, anything, anything at all to get me away from those men. Not far from the diner was a house sitting next to a small river. I ran to it and looked for a way across. I could see fields across the river and the town just beyond that. The river wasn't very wide but the water was swift and appeared deep. I thought, "If I could get across, it would put some distance between me and the SUV guys."

Downstream, the river turned and it's tree-lined banks disappeared around a curve. Upstream, about a half-mile, was a bridge across. It was part of the main road that lead to the diner in one direction, and towards the town in the other. It was too far a run to get across, not to mention it was on the main road where the SUV guys would have to go as well. I needed to get across that river but there was no other way. No way without a cold, dangerous swim. Outside the home, I saw a couple of cars parked and I went and banged on the front door. It appeared that no one was home. I saw a dirt bike on the side of the house and thought, "That's perfect." I grabbed the handlebars and looked for a key. There was no key in the ignition. Out of panic, I gave it a couple of kick starts. Nothing happened and I tossed the bike aside. "How in the hell can I get out of here?" I could hear the revving of the SUV engine as they squealed out of the parking lot onto the main road and towards the house. They were coming my way and they'd be here in seconds.

It was then that I had an idea. I'd done it before. And, I did it successfully to the dogs. I would try and float, float myself across the river. Float just like I did in my living room. I knew that if I got across that stream, then the SUV guys would have to go all the way to the bridge to get across. That would put some space between me and them and a chance for me to get out-of-sight. So I made the decision, I stood there for a moment, and relaxed. I was trying to get the feeling but at the time I was too tense. I knew I had to focus.

I threw my pack aside and I tried again. I laid face down on the ground. I closed my eyes, and relaxed again. I exhaled and inhaled deeply several times. I made a low vibration in my throat and with my mind tried to focus within. I felt the energy start to warm my body. My eyes were closed but I could sense the earth falling underneath me. I felt my body move upward a few feet, then, I thought to myself about moving forward. I could sense that I was moving towards the river. I could feel the flow of the water in the stream moving under me. I was flying.

My eyes were usually closed but I'd occasionally open them ever so slightly to see. I could hear the screeching of tires behind me as the SUV skid to a stop where I had been standing and where I had left the pack, but I remained calm. I had moved over the river and once passed, continued over the far bank and over a freshly plowed field. I kept my eyes squinted closed to keep distractions to a minimum, but open enough to see. I saw a freshly plowed field moving past diagonally underneath me. I felt it's furrows and valleys like a vibrating moving pattern below me as I kept up my concentration. I noticed I was comfortable with a distance of about 5 feet over the ground and wasn't yet beginning to notice any fatigue. It must have been the several days of mental rest that gave me the extra energy because I felt like I didn't want to stop, at least not yet.

As I continued flying across the pasture I looked back to check my pursuers. The SUV had headed towards that nearby bridge. The SUV was way farther behind now but was traveling along the road after me at a very fast speed. I stayed relaxed and fixated, fixated only on the ground under me and the direction of the town in front of me. After another minute I looked back again. I saw that the SUV had taken another road towards me and was gaining distance even though they couldn't drive straight towards me. I felt as though I couldn't float fast enough, and not nearly as fast as a car. Somehow I couldn't will myself faster than I could run. I didn't know how.

In front of me, I saw some railroad tracks cutting across my path. Further back, the tracks continued back to the side road that the SUV pursuers were on. To my right, the tracks seemed to go around, around past the town. I thought maybe, maybe I could stop once past the tracks. I was fairly certain I'd probably be drained out of energy by then, but, still, be close enough to run the rest of the way into town. There I could evade, blend in, or find someplace to hide. And, maybe if not totally drained, I might even find a rooftop to land on.

Then with astonishment, at the precise moment, I passed over the tracks, and with a great wave of shock to my body, I could feel the heavy parallel conductors pull heavily below me. It was a magnetic surge of force. It nearly jerked me to the ground but the energy inside me seemed to increase and then flow with great power. At once, I lifted several feet and then spun to my right, sucked in by the magnetic energy to follow the rails. Although surprised, I didn't fight the sensation, I didn't lose my concentration. The dense metal rails added energy to my body. I felt the power and used it to help keep my thoughts focused on this new "feeling." I turned and centered myself between the rails and allowed them to guide me.

I was flying away. Away around the town, and the road, and railroad crossing that the SUV was on. It was exhilarating! I could sense the metal tracks below me and they seemed infinite. They felt to emit power and amplify the energy that was coming through me. I was almost laughing as I experienced the surge of energy and noticed my speed getting faster. It was a powerful discovery, and it felt like a religious epiphany.

I closed my eyes and absorbed the attraction to the rails. I felt the rush of the wind. I could feel that I had sped up and that my velocity was far beyond what an SUV on a dirt road could keep up with. I relished the feeling. It was almost like pure joy. I felt the turns and smooth curve of the tracks. First one way, then the next. It was so joyous and I willed myself to go even faster. The wind rushed by me in a deafening howl like an open window on a bullet train. I sensed I was getting far beyond the reach of any pursuer. I opened my eyes for a moment to see railroad ties moving so fast they appeared to be moving backward. I closed my eyes again and concentrated, faster and faster I employed. I wasn't fading in energy at all, and I could feel the wind getting faster in increments. I rounded another curve.

Then I felt it. A greater force. A force in front of me that was sudden and far more massive than the rails. It occurred quickly. And in a white flash, I lost consciousness.

CHAPTER 33

Cindy Town

Cindy had made it to the town with no trouble at all and without being spotted by the men in the SUV. She worked her way towards the middle of town and found a motel. She felt a little reassured that there was a police station only a block away. But she had the question in her mind of, "would they be helpful if needed? Or on the side of the SUV guys?" She walked into the motel office and saw a heavyset woman sitting behind the counter watching TV and eating something out of a bag.

Cindy, "Hi there. Do you have any rooms available?"
The heavy woman stood up while clapping the snack dust off her hands.
"Hello there darling. I'm Janice. You need a room for the night?"
She was very friendly but the country twang in her voice made Cindy think that she had probably never been anywhere outside this town in her life.
"Yes, I do. Preferably one with a really hot shower."
Janice, "Well, I think we can get you something. Where's your car? Do you have any bags? You here, by yourself?"
Cindy made up a quick answer, "My husband dropped me off. He went shopping for a bit. He should be back in a little while. Do you mind if I pay in cash?"
Janice, "No problem at all. I'll have to charge you a deposit, honey unless you want to run that on a card. You'll get it back after your stay."
Cindy, "That's fine, I'll use cash. We don't like using credit cards.

It helps us manage our finances better."

Janice, "Whatever you like honey. Here's the key, it's room 12, just around the corner."

Cindy, "Thanks so much. Is there somewhere to eat and either a bus station or taxi stop around here?"

Janice, "The bus station is 3 streets over then turn North. It's on the North end of town, next to the hospital. I can call you a taxi but depending on how far you have to go it gets pretty expensive. And the closest thing to eat is a fast food joint just down the street, but if you'd like to eat in your room the Pizza Palace is really good, and they deliver. My brother Jeff owns it, it's great."

Cindy, "OK, pizza sounds fantastic. I'm just dying for that shower."

Janice, "Here's his menu. Give him a call. Tell him Janice told you. He'll give you some free garlic breadsticks! Do you need a bus? I thought you said your husband has a car?"

Cindy, "Oh yes, we do. But he's going hunting with some friends, I'll be heading back home."

Janice, "Is he going hunting with anyone around here? I know just about everybody. Is it with the Henderson brothers? Those guys do nothing but hunt. And when they're not hunting they're talking about hunting. And, I think they don't have anything else to wear except camo gear. Nothing but camo gear, even to church!" She cackled out loud. "I went out with Bobby Henderson for a while. But that was quite a while back. Isn't it too early for hunting season?"

Cindy could tell that Janice was happy to have some company in the office, but her questions were getting a little too involved.

Cindy, "I don't know, maybe they're getting ready for it. Thanks so much for the suggestions. I'll let you know how the pizza is."

Janice, "Ok dear, I think you'll love it. It's the best in town."

With the key and pizza menu in hand, Cindy went to the room. She ordered a pizza and had a long hot shower. She put her clothes in the sink and washed them with hand soap and hung them on the closet hangers to dry. The thought of having to wear the same clothes she wore today, tomorrow, made her shudder. "Enough with the camping life." She said out loud. Cindy answered the door for the pizza delivery in a towel, but left the door latch on and paid through the door. Once the driver was gone she opened the door and brought in the pizza from the doorstep.

The pizza was great! You never know what to expect in a small town but sometimes you can get a good surprise. After the hot shower, hot pizza, and with clothes drying, she laid down and started to watch a movie. It wasn't a minute before she fell asleep.

In the morning she woke up, stretched, and noticed how empty the room was. She got up and checked the dryness of the clothes. All was dry enough to wear. As she dressed she had thoughts of Matt sleeping out in the woods, all by himself. How nice it would have been to have him spend the night here. He would have loved the pizza too. She wondered when he would call once she got back to the city.

After visiting the fast-food restaurant for breakfast, Cindy walked the three streets over and went to the bus station at the North end of town. She inquired about a fare to the city and found that they didn't have a run that day but they did have one the next. She left the station and conceded that she'd have to spend another day in this small town.

She went back to the motel to confirm the room for another night. She walked into the office and there was another clerk there at the counter. "Oh, Hi there. Is Janice off today?" The clerk said, "Yep, she's got the afternoon and evening shift. She's off right now. How can I help you?" "I wanted to let you know I'll be needing my room for another night. It's room 12." The clerk said, "Let me check. Umm, there you go, no problem, you're all set." "Thanks so much," Cindy replied, "And tell Janice that her brother's pizza is great!" "Pizza Palace?" Said the clerk, "Yeah, it's pretty good. Have a good day." Cindy left the office and thought, "I might as well do some window shopping. Maybe I can get another outfit to wear for tomorrow's bus ride."

Cindy found some casual clothes in a small hardware shop in the center of town. And, for a second, considered looking through the display of camo wear right next to the rack of women's tops and jeans. "That would be hysterical," She thought. "Me showing up with hunting clothes. I could just see the expressions." She laughed out loud.

With her bag of new clothes in hand, she came out of the store and headed towards the direction of the motel. No sooner had she walked out the front door she saw a black SUV parked not ten feet from where she stood. She lowered her head, turned left, and walked as casually as possible although she was internally rattled by the SUV being just a few feet away. At the corner, she rounded the building and began a full run. She sprinted to the next corner and was about to make a left to head down the next street. As she rounded the building she looked back to see if anyone was following her. She was running, looking back, turning the corner when she tripped on an uneven, jutting up piece of sidewalk. She stumbled, and her next step took her directly into a fire hydrant. Her foot smacked solidly into the immobile mass of metal with the same force a punter takes when trying to punt a field goal. Immediately, she collapsed to the sidewalk.

Right away, several ladies came pouring out of a beauty salon that was there on the corner. One had dozens of shiny metal ribbons in her hair and a plastic cape on. "Oh honey, we saw you fall. Are you ok?" Cindy was on the ground in tears and her foot was in agony. "Come on inside." They helped Cindy hop into a salon chair where one of the stylists got a foot soaking bucket and poured in water and ice. She sat there soaking for a while with the ladies circled around wondering who this stranger was in their town. "Oh my goodness dear, where were you going in such a hurry?" "Just out shopping," was Cindy's quick reply. Cindy thought for a minute and realized that it had been a few minutes since she had seen the SUV. She was thinking that they probably, and apparently, hadn't noticed her. That thought made her a little angry. She was in all likelihood running for nothing and now her foot was throbbing and swelling. "What's your name hon? Where you from?" The ladies asked.

Cindy said, "I'm Cindy. I think I may have sprained or fractured my foot." The woman with the silver hair ribbons said, "Oh girl, we have to get you to the hospital." Then one of the ladies introduced herself, "Cindy, I'm Gladys. I'm a nurse." Cindy responded, "I'm a nurse too." Gladys said, "Oh really? Well, how about that. I guess we're birds of a feather. Dear, it looks pretty bad and it's swelling a bit. I can get my hair done another day. Let me take you to the hospital." Cindy said, "Oh that would be so nice of you, are you sure? I don't want to interrupt your day. But, I think it does need to be looked at. I'll probably have to have it immobilized." Gladys responded, "Dear, it's my pleasure. Now, let's get you to my car."

Gladys and Cindy went to the hospital and with Gladys's help, Cindy got her foot looked at right away.

Cindy came out of the examination room wearing a plastic foot brace and sporting a brand new crutch. As Cindy came out, Gladys had stayed and was talking with some of her co-workers. She asked, "How are you doing honey? Did they get you all fixed up? Can I take you home?" Cindy said to Gladys, "Oh you've already done so much. Are you sure you don't mind? I'm staying at the motel." Gladys said, "It's no problem at all, us nurses have to stick together."

On the drive to the motel, Gladys asked, "Where are you from? Which hospital do you work at?" Cindy answered, "I live in the city. I work at St. Dymphna General." "Oh my!" Gladys recognized the name. "That's the big one. They keep you pretty busy over there?" "Oh yes. It stays pretty busy. We call it Disaster General." They both laughed. "It's about time I need to be getting back there." Said Cindy. "What puts you in this neck of the woods doll?" Asked Gladys. Cindy answered, "My boyfriend's friend has a cabin not far from here. We took ourselves a little get-away for a few days. He wanted to stay longer, but I need to be getting back. I'll be heading back tomorrow." "Oh dear, you guys aren't fighting or anything?" "Oh no, nothing like that. He works his own schedule and I've already taken too many days off." "Good for you. I don't think they realize how hard we work. I could use a few days off myself." Said Gladys. Cindy continued, "You got that right. But, I do love it. But now, I'm ready to get back to work. I'm taking the bus home tomorrow and I'm looking forward to being at home too."

Gladys then surprised Cindy with, "Dear, I tell you what. Don't you worry about that bus. I'm going to take you. I've got the weekend off and I think I'll take my daughter into the city to do some shopping. The stores here are dreadful! It'll be great to have some girl time with my daughter. She's going to college next semester and we can get her some new things. We'll make a weekend out of it!" Cindy remarked, "Gladys, that's so kind. I don't want to impose, you've already helped me so much." "Never you mind, now I'm excited!" Gladys said smiling.

Gladys dropped Cindy off at the motel and arranged to pick up Cindy mid-morning. The following morning Cindy checked out and sat outside the motel office waiting for Gladys to pick her up. She began thinking it may be better to go to Mike's place instead of heading home. She imagined the SUV guys might be staking out her place. It might be better to call Mike and see how things were going and wait for Matt to call.

Cindy turned on her phone, "Hi Mike, it's Cindy. How are you doing? Mike answered, "Cindy! Hey! Are you and Matt OK?" Said said, "We're fine. I'll be heading back today. Did those guys harass you?" Mike excitedly replied, "Hell yeah they did! I did what Matt suggested, drove the other way and those guys found me and boxed me in with their SUV's. They questioned me and made some threats but eventually let me go. I was scared shit-less." Cindy replied concerned, "Oh my! But you're ok now?" Mike responded, "Yep. I haven't seen them since but it's only been a couple of days. And... holy-cow, I've got some stuff to tell you. But, right now I have to go. They're telling me I have to go on. It's my time." Cindy questioned, "Ok Mike, but first, can I come to your place?" Mike's short answer was, "Sure, later, I'll be there. I've got to go. Bye!" Mike hung up abruptly and left Cindy wondering why Mike was so busy. At least it seemed that the government guys were leaving him alone. And for that, she was relieved.

Cindy waited several hours in front of the motel office waiting for Gladys. She was beginning to think Gladys was going to be a "no-show" and that she may have even missed the bus run for that day and would be spending yet another night in this dinky town. Right when it seemed that Gladys was certain to be a no-show, she came pulling up to the motel. "Oh my dear, I'm so sorry. We're so running late. We couldn't decide what to pack and my husband was giving me the third degree. But he'll be alright. He can make his own dinner for once. Ha! And this here is my daughter, Jessica. She's our college-bound girl." Cindy greeted, "Hello Jessica, nice to meet you. And, congratulations." Jessica, replied, "Nice to meet you too." Gladys chimed in, "She says she wants to be a nurse like her mother, but we're trying to talk her into going to medical school. She needs to be a doctor!" "Oh mom," Jessica moaned. Gladys mentioned, "Well, we'll see. Now before we head out I need to stop by the hospital to get my check. And my friend Doris owes me too. We're going to need some spending money!"

CHAPTER 34

The Awakening

I woke up in bed. I was by myself. As I sat up it was near pitch-black but some spikes of light shot through the curtains. I said to myself, "Holy crap, my head hurts, and my shoulder is killing me." I tried moving my right arm in a circle but felt resistance around the upper arm and chest. It was hard to breathe. "Fucking hell. What a crappy night... Hello Irma." The Irma clock responded, "Hello." "Time?" I asked. "It's 10:10 am." "Oh Gawd, did I oversleep? I feel like shit." I continued out loud, "And it's hot in here. My head feels hot. What the hell day is it?"

There was just enough light to see as I stood up, then moved towards the bathroom. I nearly stumbled as I steadied myself on the dresser. "Damn," I said. I made my way to the bathroom, slowly. My head was hurting so bad I thought the mere presence of air moving past would hurt. "What the kind of crappy dream did I have this time?" Even the thought of thinking seemed painful. I stood by the bathroom window and began to take a morning pee.

I stood there for a moment trying to stay balanced and keep aim. Then, I heard a commotion outside the window. The window was open, but just a crack, and I pushed it wider to get a better view. There, outside, in the street and across the road were dozens, possibly even up to a hundred people. I could see a couple of TV vans and closer to the house a few policemen. "What the hell?" I jerked my head back to keep from being seen while peeing and finished my ritual. "What the hell is going on out there?" I wondered. I made my way to the bathroom sink and looked into the mirror. I saw a white gauze bandage going around my head. I picked at it a little and it felt worse, more painful, especially on my upper forehead. "That helps explain the raging headache. Damn, on my chest too?" Wrapped around my chest and right shoulder was another wrap of gauze. "And that explains why my arm and chest feel so tight. But, why do I have these dressings anyway?"

I walked out of the bathroom and made my way to the living room. There, I saw Cindy asleep on the couch. She was wearing tight jeans and a camouflage T-shirt. She looked cute. Oh geez, was she in my dream last night?" If my head was clearer I would have been more concerned that she was out here in the living room asleep. As I walked in she woke. "Hey babes. You're up! How are you feeling?" She asked. I told her. "I feel like crap. Absolute crap. And I've got the most massive headache. I think I had a really bad nightmare, the worst ever. I can't think clear enough to remember, but I think it was about flying, again. Do you know why I have these wraps on?" "Oh babes, let me make you some coffee.' As she got up she said, "Here, first, have a seat on the couch. Look up into my eyes." I sat down then stared into her beautiful green/brown eyes. She looked carefully in one, then in the other, and said, "That looks good, no twitching, no dilation." Then she started checking my bandages. I complained, "Ow, stop it." "Ohhkaaay!" She responded and then she started towards the kitchen with a limp. "Hey, what's up with your limping?" "Oh, it's nothing." She said, "I hurt my foot but it's not bad, really not that bad at all." From the kitchen, she asked, "How's your shoulder?" I answered, "It's sore but it doesn't hurt nearly as bad as my head."

Cindy was empathetic, "I'm sorry. Maybe some coffee and breakfast will help. Oh yeah, I've got to send Mike a quick message." Cindy stopped making breakfast for a minute and got on her phone and started texting. "What are you texting Mike for?" I asked. "He wanted me to text him as soon as you woke up." "OK, whatever," I responded. Cindy continued, "You've had a rough couple of days." "I have?" I questioned. "All I know is, I'm groggy, super hungry, and I had an awful night." "I'm so sorry babes. It'll be ready in a minute." she sympathized from the kitchen.

"I think I had another nightmare that I was falling, but it was different, like, it made me blackout. I don't remember where we were yesterday. You say it's been a rough couple of days?" I asked. She answered with, "Yeah, it's been about two days. You've been sleeping. I've been here to make sure you're OK." "Wow, watching me sleep, that sounds pretty boring," I commented. "It's way more exciting than that babe," Cindy explained.

Then I said, "By-the-way, I love your shirt." When Cindy got up I could see that her camo T-shirt had writing on it, "Real Men Marry Girls Who Wear Camo." She pulled at her shirt to look at it and started laughing. "So you like it?" I knew it was her idea of a funny joke. "Yep, love it. You should wear camo clothes every day." I think she was proud she made a joke because it was not something that she'd ever wear. She was a girly-girl and always liked to dress the part. I appreciated that. The joke was a good one.

"Mike should be here in a little while. You relax on the couch and have your coffee. Can I get you something for your head?" "Sure," I answered. "Anything would help." She went into her purse and found some headache pills. "When Mike gets here we'll fill you in. Do you remember anything?" "Not really, just bits and pieces. Everything is a blur." "Well, that's Ok. Just sit, relax. And don't worry. I think everything is going to be all right. Just like you said it would. I've got to make some calls."

Right then I remembered seeing all those people outside. I asked her, "What are all those people doing out there? Did someone get shot or something? I always thought this was a pretty safe neighborhood." She came over, kissed me on the forehead, and said, "Wait for Mike. He'll tell you everything." And with that, she went to the bedroom to make her calls. I sat there on the couch, drinking coffee, snacking on eggs and a sausage biscuit, and waiting for my head to clear. Cindy was in the bedroom and was chatting away. After some food and coffee, I was feeling better, although a bit drowsy again so I laid down and proceeded to take a nap.

It couldn't have been but a few moments later when I woke up to the commotion of Mike bursting in the front door. He was dressed sharper than usual. I thought he finally must have bought some new clothes. "Matt! You're up! How are you doing? Good? How's your head? Did you see all the people out there?" He had way too much energy for me to cope with at that moment. "Woah there. Ease up on the questions for a minute. I still feel half asleep." I said. Mike started pacing back-and-forth around the room then said, "Ok, sorry about that, but I have so much to tell you." I responded, "Mike, that's all well-and-good but hold up, just give me a minute." Cindy had heard Mike's entrance and came back into the living room. "Hey Mike," Cindy greeted. "How's he doing," Mike asked. "Everything looks to be fine." Cindy answered."Great, that's awesome. Have you talked with him about anything?" Asked Mike. Cindy said, "No, not yet. He's only been up a little while." Mike then asked, "Mind if I have one of those coffee's?" "Sure thing." Cindy went to fetch Mike a coffee. At that moment, I thought coffee was probably the last thing he needed.

CHAPTER 35

The Time Between

Mike sat down next to me and asked, "How are you feeling?" "Pretty shitty, but feeling better," I replied. "I can't remember what happened last night. I feel like I smashed my head and whacked my arm falling down some stairs. I can't remember though." Mike asked, "What's the last thing you remember?" I told him, "I think I remember, flying? But, I think I was dreaming that." Mike said, "I don't know what you were dreaming, but I think maybe we should start with what you can recall last. Do you remember being at the cabin?"

Cindy came back in with a coffee for Mike and sat down. "The cabin? Oh yeah, that was great by-the-way. Thanks so much. Really great!" I turned and winked at Cindy. Mike turned to Cindy and said, "Cindy, before I tell him more, do you want to tell Matt what happened to you guys after the cabin." Cindy said, "Sure. Ok, where should I begin? Umm, I remember going through the woods to that town. Ah, Matt, do you remember being chased by those dogs?" I thought for a moment. "Oh yeah... I made them float when they came around that barn." "Yep," she said, "And do you remember us separating in the subdivision just outside of town." "Yeah, we were in a bush." "Right. You went back to get those packs and I went into town." I told her, "Yeah, you did. I was worried about you. We were trying to dodge those SUV guys." I could tell that my thoughts were starting to clear.

Cindy continued with, "Right, well, I got a ride back into the city with a lady that worked at a hospital there. She is a nurse too. She's so nice. Her name is Gladys. Anyway, as I was waiting for her to pick up something at the hospital, I went in to say thanks to the people I met the day before. That's after I had hurt my foot when I tripped on the sidewalk in town. Then, just as we were leaving, we saw a farmer pull his truck into the front entrance of the hospital and we noticed he was trying to get a man out of the front seat. He said he was driving his tractor and found him lying in his field, by the train tracks. He said that when he first found him, he thought the man might be dead. He said it looked as though he was hit by a train. But, he was still breathing, so he brought him to the hospital.

Of course, right away I saw that it was you! I told Gladys I knew you. That you're my fiance'. It took some convincing not to admit you to the hospital right there but I persuaded her to take us here. I said you had a condition that makes you sleep poorly at night. Which IS true. I explained to her it's like an advanced form of narcolepsy. It's not normally serious but could cause you to fall deep asleep on some very rare occasions.
She agreed, and we gave you a quick bandage where you bumped your head, but on the way back she started to ask so many questions, I finally had to tell her the whole story. About how we were evading the SUV guys. And, how we stayed in the woods. She felt so sorry for us. I really love her. Anyway, we brought you back here and you've slept for almost 2 days. I've been keeping an eye on you. And, since we got back I've been here, waiting for you to wake up."

"Wow, I do remember camping with you in the woods." I said, "And I also camped at a campground." "You went to a campground?" Cindy said surprised. I told her, "Yeah, and then I was being chased by the SUV guys to this town, but, I recall, there was a freshly plowed field, and, and these train tracks. I think I was floating. Then, flying fast. Now I remember! I hit a train!"

Mike stood up and asked, "What do you mean you were flying?" Cindy said at almost at the same time as Mike, "You really did hit a train?" I answered them, while looking at my bandages, "I ALMOST hit a train. I noticed it and tried to get out-of-the-way but I guess I wasn't totally successful. Cindy said, "I guess you weren't. I'm glad you didn't get hurt more than you did!"

I turned to Mike, "Mike, you know how I've learned to float things? Things like the metal balls? Well, apparently, I can do that to myself." Mike's eyes opened wide. He put his hand to his chin and started rubbing. He was thinking and then started to pace quickly around the living room. Then he said out loud, "You're not kidding me about the floating? Self floating? That's GREAT!" "I guess so. It got me away from the SUV guys" I said, "What's got you so enthusiastic? And, by-the-way, I like your new clothes, but first, I've got to ask, why are we here? How come the SUV guys haven't come? Wouldn't this be the first place they'd look?

Mike sat down again and began to tell his story.

"Let me tell you what's been going on. You remember when we left the cabin and I tried to take those guys off your trail?" "Oh yeah, Mike. I was worried about you. What happened?" I asked. "Those guys took the bait. They came after me, stopped me, and harassed me. I thought they were going to take me to jail or whatever place that they were going to send you. But, after a while, they let me go." "Well, that's good," I told him. He said, "It is. But when I got back in the city I took the laptop and did what you told me to do." I scolded him, "But Mike, I told you to do that only if circumstances got extreme." Mike said, "Well, I thought they were pretty extreme."

Cindy asked Mike, "Mike, what did Matt tell you to do?" Mike answered, "I should have told you earlier but I've been so busy that I haven't given you all the details." "What details?" She looked suspiciously at Mike. "Matt had given me the laptop and told me that, if anything should happen, take what's on it and give it to the newspaper." Cindy asked, "Why take the laptop to the paper? What IS on it?" I took over the story and started explaining to Cindy, "Cindy, I thought if anything happened, if say, they took us away, then Mike would take the laptop to the media and they might print an article, or start their own investigation. Maybe get people or the police involved. Then, hopefully, someone would come rescue us. Then they'd have to release us. Or, at least know that we've been taken." Cindy inquired, "Why, what's on the laptop?" I told her, "I basically put on it what's happened to us, a timeline of what's gone on, as well as the videos that we took at home and some copies of the videos we took at Dr. J's office. And, I wrote a short manifesto that stated that if this has been found, it's because we've been taken against our will." "Oh, ok." She turned to Mike and said, "Mike? When were you going to tell me this?" "I didn't think it mattered, and I have been pretty busy," said Mike. "But the response has been Un-be-lieve-able!"

I asked Mike, "What response?" "Come over here," Mike said as walked us over to the living room window. He opened the curtains and we looked out. We could see dozens of people, police, and TV vans. "You see all this? This is all for you!" I asked Mike, "What do you mean, this is all for me?" "I mean, all these people, they're here because they know about you. They know what's happened and they want to meet you. They're concerned, or supporters, or, some are just curious." When the crowd saw us looking out the window, several started waving and I saw someone lift a homemade sign that had "Show Us" in big letters written on it. Another had a sign that said, "Freedom is A RIGHT." We quickly closed the curtains and sat back down.

I asked Mike, "So, you're saying that the story went out in the paper?" He explained, "Yeah, it did. It went out in lots of places. Your story is everywhere!" I responded with a bit of shocked amazement, "Wow, Mike. What did you do?" He responded, "Well, when I got back here I figured that, if it was a good thing that one paper knew what was going on, then more would be even better. That day, I went to two different papers. At first, they thought I was just a crack-pot but when I showed them the videos, they wanted to know everything! And, the next day I sent it to three other news outlets and made a social media page and uploaded a video or two. Since then, my phone has been ringing off the hook. Everyone wants to know! The videos have gone viral! The other day I was even interviewed on TV." I could see that Mike was extremely proud of himself. Then Mike added, "I think that, with all the people that know what's going on, and with all this publicity, those government guys have had to back off. I mean, how could they do anything with all these people watching?"

I sat there amazed by Mike's resourcefulness and entrepreneurial spirit.

He then continued, "Over the past few days I've received tons of requests for talk shows and interviews. I couldn't even answer all the questions they were asking, and they want us to come back! Isn't it exciting? How's that for being a manager?" They're ready to interview you right away when you feel up to it, that is. When do you think you'll be ready to start? I've got all kinds of ideas. They'll probably want us on Oprah too. I'll take care of it all. This is going to be great! We can start that roadshow. What do you think?"

"Holy shit Mike." This was quite a lot of information for me to process, I sat there thinking for a moment. Then I told him with some humility, "Mike, at first I was angry at you. All this time, I've been trying to keep this a secret and you've done the exact opposite. But, now that I think about it, you may have done the best thing possible. You say the government guys haven't bothered you at all?" "Nope, not a bit." He answered. "And you, Cindy, no problems?" She said, "No Matt. Not at all. Even my department manager called me and said I can come back whenever I want." I was happy for her, "Wow, that's even better than

I thought. No worries about your having to find a new job then? She responded happily, "Nope, it's all good."

Then there was a knock at the door. Cindy got up to answer. It was Dr. J. He came in pronouncing, "It took a little doing to get past the policeman outside, but once I told him I was your doctor, he let me through. I told him that he looked like a teeth grinder and asked if he was. I asked if it was keeping him up at night. Anyway, he's having an appointment at my office tomorrow." Dr. J gave a big laugh. He then turned towards Mike, "Hello, again Mike. Thanks for giving me a call." He greeted Mike, and they shook hands.

Dr. J then turned and asked me, "How are you doing Matt? How's my favorite patient? Are you sleeping well?" he was smiling profusely. I told him, "It's good to see you. Yeah, I'm feeling alright. I've had a severe headache this morning but it seems to be going away. According to Cindy, I've slept for almost two days." He answered, "You must have been exhausted. And missing meals can often trigger migraine headaches, not to mention severe blows to the head." He laughed again as he pointed at my bandages. "I hope you've had something to eat. But, I would suggest you stay away from cheese. It has a compound that often causes migraines or makes headaches worse." I said, "I haven't had any cheese but Cindy did make me some breakfast," "That's good." Dr. J responded, "What do you think of all the attention?"

I said, "It's impressive. But, I haven't had to deal with it yet. And, I'm not sure what to think." Dr. J said, "Yes, I understand. I think Mike has done a good job of getting the word out. Before all this, I was asked by Dr. Ebb, that is, I was commanded to release your case. But only yesterday, he called me to say that he had been reassigned and that I should continue on with your studies and testing. I think his "higher-ups" weren't liking the media attention. Anyway, the short of it now is, I'm going to be your attending physician if you'd like, that is. I want to continue monitoring you. You know, make sure you are both physically well and mentally healthy."

"That sounds great Dr. J. I'm glad you're back in the loop. I can't wait to get back to a more normal life." I told him. Dr. J said, "It appears you and Mike here have created quite a sensation. And, that's not the half of it, this very morning, I've been asked to speak at the sleep conference next month in Tampa. That's the "Big One" for my profession. I hope I can give them a good speech. You know, not put them to sleep!" Dr. J laughed at his joke.

Just then there was a knock at the door. Mike answered and a policeman asked, "The news reporters heard that Matt was seen and they would like to have an interview. Maybe that would help get these people to go home?"

Mike turned to me and asked, "What do you say, Matt? Want to say a few words?" I thought for a minute then said, "Sure, why not. Let me get some decent clothes on." I changed into something more presentable and put a hat on to cover my bandaged head. The officer then lead us all out front. Right away, two cameramen and reporters came running from across the street and the crowd of people became excited and started to gather. The officers kept them at a distance as the news camera's focused in. We were immediately barraged by questions. There were just too many to answer, so we stood there silently, waiting for a break in the interrogations and noise.

Eventually, Mike raised his hands and slowly, then finally, the questions stopped. We stood in the middle of the crowd and in the brief silence one man yelled, "Show us!" Then, one of the reporters copied his request and said into the microphone, then pointed it at us,.Matt, can you show us what you can do?" I turned and looked at Cindy, then Dr. J and Mike. They just looked back at me.

I reached into my jacket pocket and pulled out one of the metal magician's balls. I stretched out my arm with the ball in hand

and closed my eyes. I breathed in slow and deep and felt the weight of the ball in my palm. The reporter's camera's moved in a bit closer. The ball lifted. In that moment's silence, I slowly opened my eyes to see dozens of people's eyes wide open as they watched the ball. I levitated it up, almost 10 feet above the heads of the crowd, as I wanted to make sure everyone could see.

Then with a simultaneous gasp and roar, the crowd started clapping and whistling. I pulled the ball back and let it fall down into my hand. With that, Mike started to crowd control by saying, "That's all for now. Thank you everybody for your concern. Thank you, everyone!" He told Cindy, Dr. J and I to head back inside and said he would manage the reporters and help the police get rid of the crowd.

As we walked back to the house, I had my arm around Cindy's shoulder. Following behind, every few steps, Dr. J would pat me on the back. As we entered the house I looked back to see the crowd starting to disperse and Mike talking with the reporters. I didn't know what he was saying, but at that moment I didn't care. Once inside, Dr. J shook my hand one more time, rather vigorously. "Matt, I'm glad you're doing fine, and we'll be in touch. Right now I've got a presentation to work on! I'll see you later in the week or whenever you're ready. You let me know. You two have a great day." And with that, he left.

In the middle of the living room, I turned to Cindy, gave her a hug, and asked, "Well, what do you think?" With smiling eyes, she looked back into mine and said, "I think everything is going to be all right." Then we kissed. After our kiss, I said to her, "You know, I think it's going to be better than all right. I think things are going to be great!" Then she said, "Well, you know it's not going to be the same anymore." I told her with a hint of a joke about Mike, and also feeling much more relaxed about the whole situation, "That's for sure. But, with you here with me, and Mike on the case, I'm not the least bit worried. I can see everything's going to be just fine." She took a step back from me and crossed her arm's, squinted her eyes at me, and asked, with a bit of sarcasm, "Oh yeah? And what? Are you starting to see the future now, too?"

"Maaaybee." I told her with a sly grin. She looked back at me with smiling eyes. I then took her hand and started to lead her towards the bedroom. "Hey, would you like to see a magic trick?"

THE END (For now.)

INSIDE LOOK

Below, I've listed actual items or real occurrences that are referenced in the book.

* St Dyphnya – Patron saint of mental disorders

* Dreams of floating – randomly occurred to me as a boy for years

* Nighttime demon-sweep – I did this as a boy

* Planned 1st date at home night – a real dating experience

* Igor Sikorski – Aviation pioneer, founder of Sikorsky Aircraft Corporation, and his deja-vu experience as mentioned in several accounts

* Neil Strauss – author of "The Game"

* Mike "pea-cocking" in suit and tie – a friend's actual experience

* Bar scene with "Coffee" – entire evening happened as written with myself and a friend

* Keegan's – a real Irish bar in Atlanta

* Pineal Gland – actual brain organ. Function undetermined.

* Levitating Bottle Cap illusion – can be bought online

* "The Cube" personality test – instructions can be found online

* $1,000,000 challenge by James Randi – is no longer available

* Junior Chambers of Commerce (JAYCEES) – Chapters can be found in almost every city

* Cheese can sometimes trigger headaches – Tyramine

* Raymond Bishop - Priest involved in 1949 exorcism of a St. Louis boy

* Saint Bosco – Patron saint of Magicians